PURRFECT GRAN

THE MYSTERIES OF MAX 85

NIC SAINT

PURRFECT GRAN

The Mysteries of Max 85

Copyright © 2024 by Nic Saint

All rights reserved. No part of this book may be reproduced in any form by any electronic or mechanical means including photocopying, recording, or information storage and retrieval without permission in writing from the author.

This is a work of fiction. Names, characters, places, brands, media, and incidents are either the product of the author's imagination or are used fictitiously. The author acknowledges the trademarked status and trademark owners of various products referenced in this work of fiction, which have been used without permission. The publication/use of these trademarks is not authorized, associated with, or sponsored by the trademark owners.

Edited by Chereese Graves

www.nicsaint.com

Give feedback on the book at: info@nicsaint.com

facebook.com/nicsaintauthor
@nicsaintauthor

First Edition

Printed in the U.S.A

PURRFECT GRAN

A grandmother is like a grand-angel

Lately things had been going swimmingly for us, so I should have known that it wouldn't last. It all started when Dooley decided to feed a bird, and that bird decided it was a good idea to bring along all of his friends and family. Odelia wasn't happy about it, but Gran immediately saw an opportunity to make some money. And then there was the brain surgeon who came to stay with us. Before long, the man was running for his life and accusing Gran of trying to murder him. I could have told him this was par for the course with Vesta Muffin: kind, sweet-natured and loving. Until the gloves come off.

CHAPTER 1

Dooley had been idly watching a butterfly ascend into the blue cloudless sky when he thought he noticed something that was a little out of the ordinary. Up there, in the tree that provided him and his best friend Max with some much-appreciated shade, a bird was sitting and looking at him intently. Most birds, when they notice a cat nearby, either flee or make sure the cat can't get at them in any way, but this bird just sat there, and if Dooley wasn't mistaken, there was a certain arrogance in the bird's attitude. A certain 'come and get me if you can' kind of thing going on.

"Look at that bird, Max," he said therefore, giving his friend a nudge in the pudgy midsection.

"Mh," said Max, reluctant to open his eyes as he had been resting happily and even snoring a little.

"That bird. You have to see this, Max."

Max opened one eye and regarded him blearily. "I was sleeping," he announced, as if Dooley hadn't been able to ascertain that for himself.

"Look at that bird, Max," he said, and pointed at the creature in question.

Finally, Max decided that adhering to his friend's request might be the best way to shut him up and looked where Dooley was pointing.

"It's a bird," he said finally.

"I know it's a bird, but will you look at his face."

"I've looked at his face," said Max. "Now can I go back to sleep, please?"

"I think he wants something," said Dooley. "As if he's angry with us or something and he wants to duke it out. I've never seen a bird look at a cat like that before, Max. Do you think we should engage?"

"Do not engage," was Max's advice. "Just lie back and close your eyes. You'll see that when you wake up again, the bird will be gone."

"Imagine if he were looking at Brutus like that," said Dooley. "He's spoiling for a fight, Max. Actually spoiling for it."

"It's just a bird, Dooley," said Max. "Let it go."

Dooley certainly thought that Max's words made perfect sense. But try as he might, the way that bird just kept staring at him—without blinking no less!—was getting on his nerves. Usually a very placid sort of cat, he didn't like it. It unnerved him. It got under his skin. Which quite possibly was exactly what that bird was looking for. In other words: psychological bird warfare!

"I'm going up there to talk to him," he said now.

"Don't go up there, Dooley."

"I'm going up there."

"Don't— And he's gone."

Too right he was gone. He couldn't let this pass. If this bird wanted something from him, let him come right out and say it. All these psychological games he was playing didn't sit well with Dooley at all.

And so he was up and climbing that tree before Max could stop him. Even if Max had wanted to stop him, he couldn't have, since Dooley had always been the more nimble of the duo, with Max easily twice or even three times his size, and gravity works very hard on those who don't monitor their food intake—though Max would argue that it was his big bones that were to blame.

He had fully expected the bird to take flight the moment he placed his paw on that tree, but instead, it just kept sitting there, looking at him in a sort of curious way, as if he didn't understand that when a cat climbs a tree and approaches a bird, it usually spells bad news for the bird.

Maybe he isn't very clever, Dooley now thought. Maybe his parents haven't told him that he should be careful around cats—the natural hunters of the animal kingdom. Or maybe he's one of those birds that have grown up in an environment free of threat. Kept safe and out of harm's way. Coddled and spoiled rotten. And this was the end result: a bird who put himself at unnecessary risk because he simply didn't know any better.

"Dooley, what do you think you're doing?" asked Max, who had finally decided to get up from his resting place and now stood underneath the tree, watching Dooley's progress with a look of concern on his face.

"I'm going to talk to this bird," said Dooley. "He's clearly spoiling for a fight, and I'm going to bring the fight to him."

"But Dooley, you're not a fighter," said Max.

He knew that. Of course he knew that. But this bird had gone too far. And so he should be taught a lesson in humility and appropriate behavior.

He had finally reached the limb where the bird was seated

and approached the winged creature in a slow and what he hoped was an unthreatening fashion. It wouldn't do for that bird to fly off now and leave Dooley sitting high up in that tree with no way to get down again without the assistance of a firefighter or Chase Kingsley, his human's husband.

"Okay, so what do you want, bird?" he asked, deciding to go for the tough-cat approach. "You talkin' to me? You talkin' to me?!"

The bird just kept right on staring at him.

"Am I wearing something of yours?" He had heard this line in a movie and thought it sounded pretty neat. And since cats don't wear clothes, and neither do birds, it was also ironic. Though it could have been sarcastic or cynical. He never knew the difference between these three forms of humor.

"Who are you?" asked the bird, and contrary to what Dooley had surmised, he didn't actually look all that arrogant or belligerent now that he saw him up close and personal. Quite the contrary. He looked… curious.

"Oh, I'm Dooley," he said, feeling as if the bird had taken the wind right out of his sails. He wasn't angry with the bird anymore, and now wondered why he had ever thought that it was challenging him to a duel. "I live here," he added. "And that's my friend Max down there. He also lives here. In fact, we both live here," he said, in case he hadn't made his meaning clear.

"I'm Stewart," said the bird. "And I'm looking for a place to stay."

"You don't have a home to go to?" asked Dooley, who hated when that happened.

"I'm lost," said the bird, and gave a very good impression of a sad bird all of a sudden, going so far as to slump a little and cocking its little head to one side and regarding Dooley in a piteous way that touched his heart.

"Where are your mom and dad?" he asked, figuring this must be one of those birds that had fallen out of the nest and couldn't find their way back home.

"I don't have a mom and dad," said the bird, and Dooley actually placed a paw on his chest at this.

"Aw, but that's so sad," he said. And so he yelled out to his friend, who was still on the ground and looking up at him with a look of concern on his face. "The bird doesn't have a mom or dad, Max. And he doesn't have a home to go to."

"Be that as it may," said Max, "I think you better get down from that tree now, Dooley."

"In a minute," he said. "What did you say your name was, little buddy?"

"Stewart," said the bird. "Could I…" He cocked his head to the other side now, a cute gesture. "Could I stay with you for a while, Dooley? You seem to have a nice home, and you and Max seem to be good people. Otherwise, I wouldn't ask."

"But of course!" he said, glad that he could help. "Of course you can stay with us. We have very nice humans, and I'm sure they'll only be too happy to put you up for the night —or fortnight—or longer if that's what you need."

He now glanced down and wondered how he was ever going to get out of that tree. Stewart didn't have such qualms. He simply flew down, and as he took position on the top of Max's head, he said, "Hi, Max. My name is Stewart, and your friend Dooley has been so kind to invite me to stay with you guys from now on. I'm sure we'll all be great friends. Now, can you please show me my new home? I would like to get acquainted. And could you also show me where I can have a bite to eat and some water to drink?"

"Well…" said Max, and darted a look at Dooley that the latter interpreted as not all that happy with the invitation that he had offered to the tiny bird. But since Max was essentially a kind-hearted cat, he decided to show Stewart where he could stay and where he might find something to fill that tiny tummy of his. And as Dooley watched with a smile as his friend walked into the house with the bird still perched on top of that large head of his, it suddenly dawned on him that he was stuck in a tree—and not for the first time!

CHAPTER 2

It was a pitiful sight to see such a tiny creature, and an orphan, no less, without a home to go to, sitting alone in that tree. And so I fully understood now why Dooley had found it necessary to offer it a place in our home. I wasn't sure whether Odelia would agree with the judgment call my friend had made. But then Odelia is nothing if not a lover of all creatures great and small, and so I was fairly confident that she would rise to the occasion and be happy that she could do her little all to bring some happiness into a life that must have been very lonely and sad indeed.

"Stewart, this is your new home from now on," I said therefore, and spread my paw to encompass the entirety of the living room, the kitchen, and the television nook. "There's also a basement," I further explained, "a second floor with a master bedroom and a spare room and a bathroom and also an attic. All in all a nice home and I'm sure you'll feel very happy here."

"Where is the food?" asked Stewart as he turned his little head this way and that in a highly-strung sort of way.

"Dooley said there would be food. So where is it? I don't see any food, Max. Where is the food?"

I smiled an indulgent smile. "Where are my manners?" I asked. Obviously this little bird was starving. "Right now, all there is to eat is what's left in our bowls, but as soon as Odelia—"

The words hadn't been fully spoken, before Stewart was already flitting to my bowl and landing right on top of the remnants of kibble that were in there. Before I could say more, he was gobbling pellet after pellet in a way I hadn't seen before with any living creature, whether bird or other pet. How he did it, I didn't know, but he managed to stow away at least ten of those little nuggets. For such a tiny creature, that was unheard of—at least by me.

"I see you like that, don't you?" I said. "And the moment Odelia and Chase arrive home from work, I'll tell them that they have to stock up on bird food." Since I knew that birds adhere to a different diet than cats, I figured he probably was yearning for some seeds and nuts and suchlike, not the meat-heavy diet that cats like to follow.

"This is fine for now," he said. "Thanks, Max. Where is Dooley?"

It was then that I realized that Dooley was probably having a hard time getting down from that tree all by himself, and so I hurried out of the pet flap to lend a helping paw to my friend. When I looked up at the tree, I saw he was still where I had left him: stuck on the third branch from the right.

"Can you get down from there of your own accord?" I asked.

"No, Max," he said. "I cannot!" There was a hint of panic in his voice, and that was only to be understood as it's never a fun experience to be stuck in a tree. Even though after having been on the planet for a couple of million years, by now us cats should be able to come up with a solution to address this particular contingency, but apparently whatever that guy Darwin was going on about, cats haven't developed as a species. Then again, we lead pretty busy lives, and so developing a method of getting down from a tree is the least of our concerns. Also: in my experience there's usually a friendly firefighter at hand who loves nothing more than to save us from our predicament.

Brutus and Harriet now also came walking up. They had been enjoying a bite to eat next door, where they live, and as they took in the scene, Brutus had to laugh. "How many times, Dooley!" he cried.

"Yes, Dooley," said Harriet. "When will you ever learn?"

"I was only trying to help Stewart," said Dooley.

"You were trying to engage Stewart in a fight," I corrected him. Pure adrenaline had driven my friend up that tree, and that wasn't like the Dooley I knew and loved. "Maybe we'll wait for Chase to arrive home," I suggested. "He'll get you out of there in a jiffy."

"But that's going to take hours!" he lamented.

"Maybe we can ask one of the other neighbors," Harriet now proposed, taking pity on our friend. "Kurt, for instance, or Ted Trapper."

"But how are we going to get them to understand that we're dealing with a cat in a tree situation here?" Brutus asked.

"Easy," said Harriet. "We tell Fifi and she'll start barking up a storm and lead Kurt right to this tree."

"Is that how it works?" asked Brutus.

"That's exactly how it works, and why dogs always get anything done from their humans. So let's go and find Fifi, shall we?"

And without awaiting our response, she was already moving in the direction of the hole in the fence that divides our backyard from that of Kurt Mayfield, our next-door neighbor. Harriet was in luck, for both Fifi, Kurt's Yorkshire Terrier, and the man himself were sunning themselves in the backyard, along with Gilda, who lives next door to Kurt and is also the man's girlfriend.

"Fifi," said Harriet. "We need your help. Dooley is stuck in a tree."

"Oh, but of course," said the tiny Yorkie as she immediately got up from her perch in the shade of a large umbrella. "What can I do to help?"

"You can make Kurt get Dooley out of that tree," Harriet explained her grand plan.

Brutus and I had also snuck through the hole in the fence and now stood looking at our canine friend and wondering how she would go about this. One of the big mysteries of dogs that has always fascinated me is how they get their humans to do almost anything for them, and so I really wanted to see how she would get Kurt to climb a tree in his neighbor's backyard.

"Kurt," said Fifi curtly as she walked up to her human. "Dooley is stuck in a tree and you need to get him out of there."

Immediately Kurt's attention was drawn, and before our very eyes, he directed a look of concern at his doggie. "What's wrong, girl?" he said, placing his hands on both sides of her face and giving her a gentle caress. "Why are you barking like mad?"

As far as I was aware, Fifi hadn't barked like mad at all, but then I guess the canine language is interpreted differently by humans than it is by cats. To us, it had sounded merely like a simple stating of the facts, but to Kurt, there was a sense of urgency involved that spurred him into action.

"What's wrong with Fifi?" asked Gilda, who was sipping from a large cooling drink and had put on a bathing suit that was very colorful indeed. And now that I paid attention, Kurt was also wearing a similar bathing suit, only his consisted of a pair of purple Speedos that were entirely too small for him and made him look like a sausage whose casing is shrink-wrapped. Not exactly a sight for a discerning cat's sensitive eyes.

"Will you look at Kurt," said Brutus, who had noticed the same thing. "Something is about to go pop down there."

"Don't make fun of him," I advised. "He's the man who will have to save Dooley, remember?"

"I'm not making fun of the man," said Brutus. "Just pointing out an aspect of his wardrobe that is too peculiar not to comment on."

"I think she wants something," said Kurt.

"She can't be hungry," said Gilda. "She just ate."

"Maybe she's in pain? She looks very nervous all of a sudden."

Fifi now ran to the hole in the fence and then back to Kurt, and he instantly got the message. "I think she wants to show me something," he said, and hurried to the fence to see what was going on.

Fifi hadn't waited for his response but was already streaking through that hole in the fence and straight up to the tree where Dooley still sat patiently awaiting his heroic savior to come to his rescue.

Fifi now barked up a storm while standing underneath that tree and looking up at Dooley.

"Oh, it's Dooley," said Kurt. "I think he's stuck in a tree."

Gilda had also joined her partner, and the both of them stood gaping across that fence in the direction of the location where Dooley was now mewling piteously to add some urgency to his predicament.

"Will you look at that poor darling," said Gilda, whose heart bled as she took in the scene. She gave her boyfriend a gentle nudge. "Well, what are you waiting for? Go and get him out of that tree, Kurt."

"I'm sure Odelia will do it," said Kurt, who was as reluctant as anyone to risk breaking his neck for the privilege of saving a neighbor's cat from a tree. "Or Chase."

"Clearly, there's nobody home," said Gilda, whose heart is big for all of petdom, not just dogs, the species Kurt seems to favor. "Go on then. Help him!"

Kurt grumbled something, but since he didn't like to disappoint his girlfriend, he opened the little gate that allows passage from one backyard to the next, and walked up to the tree. He scratched his scalp as he looked up at Dooley.

"Now how did you go and get stuck up there, huh, little buddy?" he said.

"See?" said Fifi as she gave us a look of triumph. "What did I tell you? Kurt is like putty in my paws."

It certainly had been a master class in learning how to get your human to do your bidding, I had to admit. Even Kurt, who normally doesn't care one hoot about cats, was about to do something he would normally never do: save a cat from a tree.

"I'm going to need a ladder," he announced, and darted a hopeful look at Gilda.

"Tex has a big ladder," said Gilda. "Better go and get his."

Kurt grunted something unintelligible and stomped off in the direction of the opening in the hedge between our backyard and that belonging to Odelia's mom and dad. Moments later he returned with the ladder on his shoulder and was putting it up against the tree. Climbing it was but the work of a moment, and as we watched on with bated breath and a sense of awe, he grabbed Dooley from the tree and was carrying him back to safety within minutes.

"I thought Kurt was a retired music teacher?" said Harriet. "He looks like a retired fireman instead."

"Music teachers know all about ladders," Brutus pointed out. When we gave him a curious look, he shrugged. "Tone ladders. It's the same thing, really."

"Very funny, Brutus," I said, earning myself a grin from my friend.

"Thank you, Mr. Mayfield," said Dooley, ecstatic to be standing on terra firma once again. "Thank you so much!" and in his desire to express his gratitude not just with words but also with gestures, he actually tried to give Kurt a token of his appreciation by rubbing himself against the man's leg. Kurt didn't seem to like this one bit, but since Gilda was looking on, he tolerated it as much as he could and even gave Dooley a tentative sort of pat on the head.

"That's all right, little buddy," he said. "You're fine now. You're all right."

"Well done, Kurt," said Gilda. "You did a wonderful thing here today. Doesn't that make you feel all warm and fuzzy inside?"

"Absolutely," Kurt confirmed. "I feel very warm and very fuzzy..." He lifted his leg in an exaggerated fashion to step over Dooley, and then hurried off to return the ladder from where it came. The man had done his duty, made his girlfriend happy, and that, as far as he was concerned, was that.

He returned without giving us the benefit of his attention but simply hurried past us and disappeared behind his fence, locking it in the process just to make sure.

"That was very nice of Kurt, wasn't it?" said Dooley. Clearly, Kurt had found a new fan in Dooley, even if the retired music teacher wouldn't have enjoyed the notion if he had been aware of it. Then again: no good deed goes unpunished.

"Maybe we should sing him a song, you guys," Harriet suggested. "Just to show him how much we appreciate what he did for us." And without awaiting our input, she opened her mouth and started belting out one of her favorites: *I Am a Woman in Love* by Barbra Streisand. Whether Kurt understood the lyrics or not, the fact was that his head suddenly appeared over the parapet, and as he took in the scene, I had the impression the music teacher in him didn't enjoy Harriet's version of that perennial Barbara classic. At least if the agonized expression on his face was anything to go by.

"I think he likes it," said Dooley. "He really likes it, Harriet." And since he wanted to add his own contribution, he also opened his mouth to sing along, and so did Brutus. The only one who wasn't singing was me, but then I was watching Kurt closely, and judging from the vein that was pulsating in his right temple, I didn't want to risk being beaned by a size-fourteen shoe. And so instead of joining this impromptu choir recital, I hurried indoors to be safe from any incoming projectiles emanating from our neighbor.

When I entered through the pet flap, I was surprised to find that all of our bowls were empty. And since I couldn't imagine that one tiny bird could possibly be responsible for this, I glanced around to find the intruder. It was only when I heard a tweet that I looked up and saw that the kitchen cabinets were full of birds. And as my jaw dropped, Stewart disassociated himself from the pack and said in a proud sort of voice, "Max, meet my brothers and sisters. Guys, this is Max, the one who has kindly offered us a new home!"

CHAPTER 3

Jeff Morrison opened the hood of his rental car and stared blankly at the engine. Even though he vaguely knew that cars have engines, he had to admit that he didn't know the first thing about remedying any sort of problem with the contraption. He was a surgeon, after all, used to rummaging around in people's insides, not analyzing the innards of his own vehicle and making sure it worked as it should. And so after only a few moments, he had to declare defeat and closed the hood again with a clang.

He glanced around. He had absolutely no idea where he was, and cursed himself for not bringing along his phone charger. At least he would have had GPS and could have found his way to the nearest gas station where hopefully they could lead him to a garage that could tow his car and get it fixed. He had an important conference to attend, and since he was one of the speakers, the last thing he wanted was to get lost.

But since this car didn't seem to be able to get him to where he was going, he saw there was only one thing he could do: hitchhike. But since the area where his car had broken down didn't seem all that inhabitable, as very few cars passed by, he decided he'd better start walking in the direction he had been going and hope for the best.

He had been walking for ten minutes when the sound of a car made itself known, and so he held up his thumb and assumed the hitchhiking position. The car didn't even slow down, but instead seemed to speed up when its driver caught sight of him. And as it passed him by with a roar of its powerful engine, he wondered what it was about him that had given this person pause. He didn't think he looked all that threatening. Then again, you never know how one is perceived by other people. Maybe they took one look at him and thought he was a serial killer or some kind of dangerous drug kingpin.

He took up his walk again and had only been putting one step in front of the other for five minutes when he heard another car approaching. This time he decided to add a smile to his thumb gesture, since smiles do suggest that one doesn't pose a threat, and maybe it would make the driver reconsider the notion that here walked public enemy number one. His smile said, 'I'm just your friendly neighborhood brain surgeon, and if you give me a lift, I might even give you a free checkup.'

Unfortunately, this driver, too, had the instant reflex to stomp down on the gas pedal as soon as he took one look at Jeff.

"What's wrong with these people?" he murmured as he returned to his long walk. Soon he realized the error in his thought process. The question wasn't what was wrong with these drivers but what was wrong with him. And since self-criticism wasn't something he was familiar with, it took him a while to come up with something about himself that might make these people refuse to even contemplate giving him a lift.

He glanced down at himself and thought he looked fine enough. He wasn't wearing his suit, of course, since he had packed that for the conference. He was dressed in his casual clothes: jeans, a leather jacket, sunglasses perched on his nose, and a pair of tennis shoes. So maybe he should have worn his doctor's coat instead. People love a doctor. When they see one, they can't resist dropping their pants and pointing out the clump of hairy warts on their buttocks and ask him if he thinks it might be cancer.

"It must be the leather jacket," he determined, and immediately shrugged out of it and draped it over his arm. Now he looked like any civil servant: jeans, white shirt, and a head that was fully devoid of even a single hair. Maybe that was it. Maybe people don't trust bald men. They want to see that full head of lustrous hair, shiny and glorious. Unfortunately, this was what he had to work with, and it was probably a little late now to contemplate getting the hair transplant a colleague had been advertising. Ben Harper, who was a urologist, had had one, and he said he was getting plenty of looks from younger women again, eager to run their hands through that mighty mane. Maybe Jeff should have gone for it. Then he would have been picked up by now.

Another car came zooming past, and dutifully he stuck his hand up again. This time the driver seemed willing to give him a chance. And as he hurried to the car, which had parked on the shoulder, he bent down to take in the driver. He was surprised to see an elderly woman who gave him a curious look.

"You're a doctor, aren't you?" she said, surprising him even more.

"How... how did you know?"

"I work for a doctor," she explained. "I can smell you guys a mile away. Hop in, doc."

And even though he thought she might be an eccentric,

he decided that she looked harmless enough, and so he accepted her invitation and got into the vehicle. It was a little cramped, as it was one of those mini cars that are all the rage with city folk.

"So what kind of doctor are you?" asked the woman once she had put the car in gear and they were zooming along, too fast for his liking, he had to admit.

"Um, brain surgeon," he said.

"Oh, fancy," she said. "My son-in-law is a family doctor."

"Where are we, by the way? My phone battery died, so I have no idea."

"Next town is Hampton Cove. And the last town you must have passed through is Hampton Keys. Where are you headed?"

"Hampton Cove," he said. "I'm due to speak at a conference there tomorrow."

"I live in Hampton Cove," she said. Then she gave him a sideways glance. "You wouldn't happen to have a moment to spare, would you, doc?"

"It depends how long the moment is," he said with a smile. He was feeling more and more relaxed, figuring this woman was nice enough and would get him where he needed to be.

"It's just that my son-in-law has been acting real strange lately. I think it might be his head."

"Your son-in-law the doctor?"

"That's the one. I think he may be going bananas, but that's just my layperson's opinion, of course."

He frowned. "What are the symptoms that make you think he's losing his mind?"

"Oh, for one thing, he said I can't have a new car. And you can tell that I need a new car, can't you?" She patted the dashboard. "This baby still runs fine enough, but one of these days she's going to break down, and then where are we?"

"I have to admit that I'm not an expert on cars, Mrs..."

"Muffin. Vesta Muffin. Oh, I'm no expert either, but judging from the sound she makes I don't think she has a lot of miles left in her." She sighed. "Anyway. I asked my son-in-law for the money to buy a new car and he flatly refused to give me any. Said this car runs fine enough for my needs." She gripped the steering wheel a little tighter. "My needs! Who does he think he is, talking about my needs? As if he has even the faintest idea of what my needs could possibly be. But anyway. So I've been looking into this kind of irrational behavior and it seems to be fairly common in males like him."

"And what kind of male would that be?" he asked politely.

She waved a hand. "You know, the usual middle-aged, frustrated, unhappy male, with their careers stalled and generally a failure in life."

"Your son-in-law feels as if he's a failure?"

"He doesn't say it. But I know he's thinking it. In fact, we're all thinking it. Tex was destined for greater things, you see, but in the end he settled for the life of a family doctor, which is eating away at him." Then she seemed to brighten. "Say, do you already have a place to stay in Hampton Cove?"

He grimaced. "The organizer of the conference signed me up at the last minute, so all the hotels were full. But he said he'd try to put me up with one of my colleagues."

"How about you stay with us instead?" she suggested. "I can drive you to any conference you want. But this will give you the opportunity to study Tex from up close and personal, and then after a couple of days, you can give me your professional opinion about the guy: crazy or not crazy."

He had to admit it was an attractive offer since he didn't know the organizer of the conference all that well, and this lady seemed nice and hospitable enough.

"If I could borrow your phone for a moment, I'll talk to

the organizer," he suggested. "I got the impression he was struggling to find somewhere for me to stay but figured otherwise I wouldn't come. I'll make the suggestion to him and then if he agrees, I'll gladly take you up on your offer, Mrs. Muffin."

"Vesta, please," she said. "And what should I call you?"

"Jeff," he said. "Jeff Morrison." And as she handed him her phone, he dialed the number of Luca Adsett-Brown, the conference organizer, and moments later was in conversation with the man.

"You want to stay with Vesta Muffin?" asked Luca.

"Yes, with her and her son-in-law, who's also a doctor," he explained.

"Tex Poole," Mrs. Muffin volunteered.

"Tex Poole," he repeated.

"I know the guy," said Luca. "I probably should have invited him to be a speaker. Family medicine is going through a crisis right now, so we should collect information from as many actual family doctors as possible, and Doctor Poole is one of them."

"So do you think it's a good idea that I stay with him?"

"Absolutely," said Luca. "I think it's a great idea. You can get to know Poole and discuss things with him."

"Great," he said, well pleased. "I'll see you for the welcome speech."

And as he settled back, he thought how lucky he was to have hit upon Mrs. Muffin, who seemed like a most wonderful lady. Sweet-natured and kind. Exactly the kind of loving grandma she appeared to be. He had a feeling his stay in her home would be a great experience.

CHAPTER 4

Theo Norgrove eyed the next house closely. His little finger tingled, which was a clear sign that there might be something to grab there. His little finger never lied. "I think we should pay this family a visit." He consulted his list. "Ted and Marcie Trapper. What do you think, Taylor?"

"I think that's an excellent idea," said Taylor, pushing his glasses higher up his nose. "In fact, I think it's probably the best idea you've had all day, Theo."

They'd had a minor disagreement one hour before when checking out a home that in the end turned out not to yield anything, and of course Taylor blamed Theo, which he shouldn't have done, since it was a joint decision.

But this time they were in agreement, and so they both set foot for the door, and Theo did the honors by pressing the bell.

It didn't take long for footsteps to be heard inside the premises. While the resident made their way to the door, Theo checked the front yard. He counted no less than six garden gnomes, and if his hunch wasn't deceiving him, there probably would be a lot more in the back.

The door swung open, and a middle-aged woman of moderately attractive aspect appeared. She seemed surprised to see two men on her doorstep, both dressed in suits and looking almost like a pair of twins. She frowned and said, "I'm sorry, but we don't belong to your religion," and made to close the door again. Just before she could, Taylor held up his badge. "Taylor Broad. We work for the government, ma'am," he said.

"We work for your local IRS office," Theo clarified.

"The IRS?" asked the woman, proving herself to be the quick-witted sort.

"That's correct. We're going door to door to determine if residents of this street are up to date on their income tax."

"Oh, but we are," she said, with a smile of relief. "My husband is an accountant, you see, so he makes sure that everything is always correct."

"We counted no less than six gnomes in your front yard, Mrs. Trapper. Did you count six gnomes, Taylor?"

"I counted exactly six, Theo."

"That's what I thought."

"Yes, Ted loves his garden gnomes," said Mrs. Trapper. "He has a lot of them. More in the backyard."

"As we suspected," said Theo, exchanging a look of triumph with his counterpart.

"As we suspected," Taylor echoed, and took it upon himself to deliver the bad news. "As you may or may not be aware, Mrs. Trapper, your husband has failed to add a list of gnomes to his tax return."

"List of gnomes? What do you mean?"

"The governor, in his eternal wisdom, introduced a gnome tax last year," said Theo, balancing back and forth on his patent leather shoes. This was the best part, he felt. To watch that look of stupefaction glide over the faces of the people they hustled. "And so an extra code was added to the tax return, asking people to list the number of gnomes they have in their possession. Your tax return has no list of gnomes."

"None," said Taylor. "Not a single one."

"And so we'll have to engage in a spot check to see how many gnomes you actually have in your possession."

"And issue a fine."

"A hefty fine."

And while the lady of the house stood looking at them as if they'd lost their minds, they both stepped inside. "By the powers vested in me by the State of New York," said Theo, "we hereby instigate a thorough search of your premises to establish the presence of gnomes."

"Please step aside, ma'am," said Taylor. "Unless you want to be held in contempt."

"Let us proceed, and we'll make this as painless as possible," Theo added.

Both men made a beeline for the backyard before the man of the house could engage in an act of concealment of his gnomes, as they had experienced on previous occasions. And as they arrived, Theo knew they'd struck gold: dozens of gnomes were in attendance, and as he started counting them, he thought this must be their lucky day. For he had just glanced across the fence and had spotted another fine collection of gnomes. And he would have climbed the fence to make sure this person didn't escape detection either when something large and heavy attached itself to the seat of his pants.

When he looked down, he saw it was the biggest dog he'd ever seen.

And as he lodged a formal complaint in the form of a loud scream of dismay, he hoped the dog wouldn't include the

Norgrove family jewels in his quest to ensure that this intruder didn't take one step further.

That was the trouble with the powers vested in them by the State of New York—or, as in their case, the powers vested in them by a desire to get filthy rich by scamming people: dogs simply didn't care one hoot about such things. Theirs was a typical black-and-white view of life: friend or foe.

"Can you please ask your dog to let go?" he asked in tremulous tones.

Mrs. Trapper had appeared, and stood eyeing him with a look of censure in her eyes, her arms folded across her chest. For a moment he fully expected her to yell, 'Attack!' but in the end she didn't.

"Rufus, off," she said in a calm tone.

"Thank you," he said the moment the large dog had released his grip on his pants.

"I've never even heard of something so ridiculous," Mrs. Trapper now revealed. "A gnome tax? When was this decided?"

"It was decided," he assured her, keeping a close eye on that dog. "And voted into law. And communicated through the usual channels."

"Well, like I said, my husband is an accountant, and if he doesn't know about it, I'm pretty sure it doesn't exist." Her frown deepened. "Let me see that badge again, will you?"

And since the dog was sitting there like a sentry, he didn't feel as if it would be prudent to refuse. And so he handed her the badge.

She studied it for a moment, then shook her head. "If you don't mind, I'm going to run this past my neighbor," she said.

"Tex Poole, who is also in breach," he informed her.

"Marge Poole," the woman clarified. "As you probably know, her brother is chief of police. And he's married to the mayor." With these words, she took a picture of the badge and placed her phone to her ear.

He exchanged a glance with Taylor, and as one man, both so-called IRS agents jumped that fence to get away from the dog and the woman. As they were running in the direction of the road, leaving that unpleasantness behind, he said, "Not one word out of you, Taylor."

"This is the second time we've had to flee a scene," Taylor grumbled.

"Was it my fault?"

"Yes, it was! You chose this house!"

"You agreed!"

"Only because you told me to!"

It looked as if they would have to agree to disagree.

"If only that dog hadn't been there," he grumbled.

"New rule," said Taylor. "First, we ask them if they have a dog. Then, and only then, do we proceed. Are we in agreement?"

"We are in agreement," he said.

Unfortunately, when he looked behind him, he saw that the darn dog had followed them. And as he yelped in fear, the monster attached itself to the seat of his pants once again! There was a kind of ripping sound, a gentle pressure against the Norgrove family jewels, and then he was proceeding with his escape without the benefit of a large portion of his pants.

CHAPTER 5

It wasn't so much that I begrudged the birds a place in our home or a stab at having a steady source of nourishment but rather that I didn't enjoy the end process of their food intake in the form of bird poop. You see, unlike cats, birds have never been domesticated, and so they're not used to using a litter box to do their business. Instead, they're more the laid-back type of animal that drops their business where it falls. The end result was that our living room, kitchen, and television nook looked like a battlefield with droppings everywhere: on the table, the chairs, the sofas, the television, even the walls hadn't been spared by Stewart and his siblings, of which I counted dozens, possibly hundreds.

"Odelia isn't going to like this, Max," said Dooley, and I thought that was something of an understatement.

"This is a nightmare," said Harriet, which was a more accurate take on the situation.

"Look at all those tweety birds," said Brutus, fascinated by the sight of all of that twittering going on. "I've never seen so many tweety birds in one place." He licked his lips. "Do you think Stewart will mind if we have a few? For breakfast, I mean. There are so many of them, a few won't be missed, right?"

"Better not," I advised Brutus.

"No, pookie," said Harriet. "Birds can get vicious when they feel attacked. Have you never seen that movie, *The Birds*?"

"Such a shame," said Brutus as he eyed a particularly fat bird launching itself close to his head.

Stewart must have told his brothers and sisters that they had nothing to fear from the cats living at this particular house, for they seemed almost brazen in their attitude towards us.

"Stewart, we need to have a word," I told the bird.

Stewart dutifully streaked down and took a seat next to me. "What is it, Max?"

"When we told you that you could stay with us for the time being—"

"There was no mention of a 'time being,'" he pointed out.

"No, that was a blanket invitation Dooley extended to Stewart," Brutus said.

"Okay, when we invited you to come and stay with us, that invitation didn't extend to the rest of your family as well," I told the bird.

"Yes, we didn't even know you had a family," said Harriet. "You said you were an orphan, remember?"

"Being an orphan only refers to one's mother and father being deceased," Brutus explained, playing devil's advocate once more. "Not to any siblings. And Stewart here never said that he was an only child."

"Exactly right," said Stewart. "I never said I was an only child. In fact, I'm not."

"Yeah, we can see that," I said as I took in the disaster area that was our former lovely home.

"Look, if you want me to clear out, just say the word," said the bird with a shrug. "It's just that I was so touched when you told me I could stay here, you know. So I won't conceal the fact that I'm slightly disappointed by this sudden about-face in what I consider my great benefactor."

I shared a glance with my friends, and Dooley gave me a pleading sort of look. "We can't send him back out there, Max," he said. "It's a dangerous world out there for a bird, especially an orphan like Stewart."

Frankly speaking, I didn't think Stewart had much to fear from the world outside as much as the other way around. But then since it wasn't technically my home to begin with, I decided that it would probably be for the best if we deferred this decision on who could or could not stay with us to the actual lady of the manor.

"Odelia will be home later this evening," I told Stewart. "Let's wait and see what she has to say, all right?"

"Oh, thank you, Max," said Stewart, actually clapping his wings together with joy. "I'm sure if she's as nice as you guys have been, that she won't make a lot of fuss about a few of my siblings staying here with me. Life does get lonely without your family or friends around, don't you agree?"

I had to say that he was right on that account. But then I caught on to what he had said. "You mean this is only a portion of your siblings?"

"Absolutely. This is only the Hampton Cove clan. There's also the Hampton Keys clan, the Happy Bays clan, the Hampton Bays clan, the…"

"I think we get the message," I told him as I closed my eyes.

I had a sort of sinking feeling that we might have been nursing a cuckoo to our bosom, who would soon take over the entire house.

And as we left the kitchen via the pet flap, I felt that we

needed to confer about this insertion into our home of this clan of birds.

"Maybe we should just eat a few," Brutus suggested. "You know, as a warning to the others. In my experience, when you launch a preemptive strike, it's usually enough to get the message across."

"We're not eating Stewart or his siblings," I told Brutus in no uncertain terms.

"But we have to do something, Max," said Brutus. "They can't be allowed to stay. I mean, simply the noise. It's the tweeting that gets on my nerves."

"For me, it's the poop," said Harriet, making a face. She pointed to a part of her fur where a bird dropping had landed. "Did you see that? It pooped on me, with no regard to the sanctity of my person. Just went ahead and pooped!"

"One of them pooped on me as well," Dooley said with a sad face. He showed us the evidence in the form of a bird dropping that had landed on his tail. "It's not very nice to be pooped on, Max. Not very respectful."

Oddly enough, they hadn't pooped on me, even though some would say I form a sizable target and am very hard to miss. But then I guess it was the luck of the draw.

"We have to talk to Odelia about this," I said.

"Odelia will be mad," said Brutus. "I can tell you that right now. When humans take a cat, they do so with the understanding that the cat will keep the house free of vermin in the form of mice, rats, and birds."

"Would you call birds vermin?" I asked.

"I would, yes," he confirmed. "Not all birds, but this lot? Absolutely."

"I don't think I like it when you call Stewart vermin, Brutus," said Dooley, who was the one who had gone to bat for the birds, after all.

"I'm sorry, Dooley. But sometimes you have to call a

spade a spade. And this bunch are taking advantage of the invitation you were so gracious to extend. It's like inviting a single person into your home and ending up with his entire extended clan squatting on your property. It's not respectful."

"No, I guess I hadn't counted on Stewart bringing along his entire clan," Dooley admitted.

Brutus directed a look at me, but I cut him off before he could launch into another plea for a preemptive strike.

"No birds will be on the menu, Brutus," I said.

"Oh, all right," he said. "I'll bet Odelia will think differently, though. I'll bet that she will beg me to start thinning out that herd."

"What herd would that be?" asked Dooley, interested.

"The herd of birds, of course."

"I don't think the collective noun for birds is herd, precious angel," said Harriet. "Pretty sure it's a flock of birds."

"Herd, flock, you catch my drift."

We certainly did, and even though I didn't like his suggestion, if push came to shove we just might have to take him up on his offer to 'thin the herd.'

CHAPTER 6

Jeff Morrison wasn't sure what to expect. A friend and colleague of his, an orthopedic surgeon specializing in knee prostheses, had told him that the indigenous population of Hampton Cove was nice enough, and had even given him a couple of addresses where he could find decent grub. But he hadn't expected that the locals would be so friendly that they would immediately set him up at their home. Unless…

He darted a quick sideways glance at Mrs. Muffin, who had been talking non-stop since she had given him a lift. She didn't *look* dangerous. Definitely not psycho-killer material. But of course, the same might not be the case for the rest of her family. Maybe she was like a scout for a clan of dangerous cannibals, who would knock him over the head the moment he set foot inside their dwelling and keep him alive and feed him until he was fattened up enough to be slaughtered and turned into sausages for the family feast.

But then he shook off the gloomy thought. Vesta was a nice old lady and had invited him to come and stay with her out of the goodness of her own heart, her family was as lovely as she was, and that was all there was to it.

"So do you think your son-in-law and his wife won't be annoyed that you brought me along to stay with them?" he asked. She had given him a glimpse into her family's dynamic, and it would appear that this Tex Poole, the family doctor, was the lord of the manor and his wife ran the roost, with Vesta having been taken in by the couple after her husband died.

It was definitely a nice sentiment, he thought, and boded well for the couple's prospects in his personal opinion, as most people didn't like to put their old folks up at their own home but preferred to ship them off to some retirement institution, and preferably one on the other side of the country. Out of sight, out of mind kind of thing. Since his own dad was still practicing medicine and wouldn't think about retiring until they yanked the scalpel from his cold dead hand, that problem hadn't posed itself yet. Mom was too happy running all over town with her posse of girlfriends to even think about retirement. And even then, the last thing she'd want was to move in with her son and his wife Matilda and their three boys.

"You live your life and we'll live ours," she had said on many an occasion, and there the matter rested for now. And since Matilda's parents lived in Nevada and were in fine fettle, there was no talk yet about putting any of them up at their own home for now.

"They'll be fine with it," Vesta assured him. "Marge loves to entertain, so she'll be delighted to have you as a guest. And Tex will be most interested to have a fellow doctor staying at the house. He so rarely gets the chance to talk to a colleague. Of course he can talk to me, but that's not the same."

"Oh, you're also a doctor?" he asked. He could definitely

see her as some kind of Dr. Ruth type of person, helping people with their problems of procreation.

"Pretty much," she admitted. "I work with Tex at the office. And since working next to a doctor is almost the same as being a doctor, I help out people by giving them medical advice from time to time. You'd be surprised at the kind of problems people can face sometimes that they don't want to bother a doctor with. That's where I come in."

"So… you practice medicine without a license?" he asked, a little confused about the exact constellation of the home he was soon going to insert himself into.

"I give advice," said Vesta. "Common-sense advice, like only a person who's been running her son-in-law's doctor's practice for many years can. And also, I run the neighborhood watch, so that gives me a certain position in the community. As well as being the mother of the chief of police, who's married to the mayor, so that pretty much makes me the First Lady of Hampton Cove." She thrust out her chest, and even though he didn't see how one thing led to another, he gave her a feeble smile in return.

"Quite the responsibility," he said.

"You bet it is. I can't count on the fingers of both of my hands the number of times people walk up to me to share a little problem they're facing—whether it be of the personal, medical, financial, or police-related kind. And even though I want to help them all, I can't. I'm just one person, you see."

"I see," he said, even though he didn't.

He glanced out of the window and saw that the fields had become interspersed with the odd dwelling, and he figured they were probably close to Hampton Cove.

"This conference," he said. "Do you know anything about the location it's being held? It said on the invitation that it's going to be organized at the Star Hotel."

"Fine place. Best hotel in town."

He nodded, content with this information. "I was going to take a room at the hotel, but unfortunately, I was too late. All the rooms were gone, so I had to find a different arrangement."

"And now you've got it!" she said, and gave him a clap on the back that almost sent him toppling into the dashboard.

Hampton Cove seemed nice enough, if the houses they passed were anything to go by. He had expected a real beach town, with lots of tourists, but as he looked around, he didn't see all that many of that ilk, which probably was a good thing, while the tourist industry is good for business, it creates a lot of nuisance for the locals, who don't always like it when their town is being overrun with vacationers.

"If we have time, we can go to the beach," Vesta said now. "We've got the best beach in all the Hamptons right here in Hampton Cove. Are you a beach bum, Jeff?"

"Not really," he admitted. And he didn't think he'd have a lot of time to go to the beach, since he would be tied up at the conference. "I'm more of a mountain man. I love trekking through the mountains with Matilda and the kids. We always make it a family outing, and I like to think that our three boys have inherited our love for the mountains as well, as they never talk about going to the beach, like many kids seem to do."

"That's nice," Vesta murmured as she glanced through the windshield, her face practically plastered to the screen.

"Is something the matter?" he asked as he watched her behavior with a curious eye.

"That guy over there," she said, and pointed to a man who was crossing the road. "I used to date him, you know."

"Is that a fact?" he asked, Vesta's personal life not at all of interest to him.

"His name is Dick Bernstein. He once invited me to go on a yacht trip in the South of France with him and a friend of his. Only when we arrived, the yacht turned out to be a broken-down old wreck and had to be towed back to port." She shook her head. "Not a fun experience, let me tell you."

"No, I can imagine it wasn't."

"And that guy over there is Wilbur Vickery," she said. "I went out with him once, but he turned out to be such a nuisance I had to ditch him." She sighed. "It's not all that easy to date once you're a certain age, let me tell you, Jeff." She gave him a quick glance. "You wouldn't have any eligible bachelors in your circle of friends, would you? I mean, doctors are a real catch, everybody knows that."

"Is that so?" he said, never having heard it put in such terms before.

"And he doesn't have to be my age," she assured him. "Any age will do. I'm not an ageist."

He smiled politely, but when she gave him another urgent glance, he understood that it hadn't been a rhetorical question but that she actually wanted him to respond. "Oh, I see," he said, therefore. "Well, I do have a couple of friends who are divorced. The scourge of the age," he added with a smile. "But they all live in Seattle, so…"

"I don't mind," she said. "Long-distance relationships are my jam, Jeff. They say they don't work, but I think they do, as long as you're willing to put in the work. Especially in this day and age of Skype and Zoom, I think they can work just fine." She thought for a moment. "Okay, sign me up."

"Sign you up for what?"

"For a date with one of your doctor friends, of course."

"Oh, well, um…"

"And if any of them are in town this week, maybe we can meet in person. The Star Hotel is where I spend most of my time, you see. Me and my friend Scarlett—who is also single, by the way, and quite a catch." Then her face brightened. "Ooh, I just had the best idea ever! Why don't we make it a double date! Me and Scarlett and two of your doctor friends?"

"I'm not sure if…"

"It's a date. Let's make it dinner at the Star Hotel." She gave him another pat on the back that made him buckle a little. "I'm so glad that we met, Jeff. The universe really works in mysterious ways, doesn't it?"

It sure did, Jeff thought. And already he was starting to regret having said yes to Vesta's kind offer to put him up at her home.

CHAPTER 7

Marge had been stamping the newly arrived books and getting them ready to put on the shelves when her phone dinged. And since she was one of those people who were like Pavlov's dog the moment the phone made its intention clear that it wanted her attention, she dropped everything and picked up the device from her desk.

'You're wanted at the house—now!' the message read, and it had been sent by her mother.

She rolled her eyes. Didn't Ma know by now that she couldn't just close up the library and run home for every little problem she was having?

And so she texted back, 'What's wrong?'

The response was immediate. 'Just get here already, will you!!!'

She thought for a moment. Her mother might be eccentric, but she wasn't certifiable. At least not yet. So if she thought Marge's presence at the house was urgently needed, it must be true. And since there wasn't anyone at the library at that moment anyway, she figured she might as well pop home for a few minutes. After all, it was just around the corner from where she lived.

So she got up, grabbed her purse, turned over the Closed sign on the door, and hurried out, making sure to lock the door behind her, lest someone wanted to take off with a haul of books. Not that she thought anyone would. Thieves love to break into places to steal things, but very rarely do they steal books. Apparently, books aren't the kind of item you can monetize.

She put a pep in her step and was almost home when her phone dinged with another message.

'WHERE ARE YOU!!!! DEFCON SIX!!!!!'

She didn't think that Defcon Six actually existed. Maybe Ma was confusing it with Seal Team Six, but it definitely was clear that some emergency was taking place. She slammed into the house and yelled, "Ma, I'm home!" but if she had expected her mother to come running, she was mistaken. As far as she could tell, there wasn't anybody home.

"God, if this is some kind of joke…" she grumbled under her breath. Just then, her phone dinged again.

'NEXT DOOR!!!!'

Ma must have seen her arrive and apparently was at Odelia's place. This time her heart made a leap in her chest. If something had happened to her daughter, or, God forbid, her granddaughter… She hurried out the kitchen door and into Odelia's backyard, where she encountered her mother in quite a state. Oddly enough, she was accompanied by a man Marge had never seen before.

"Who is this?" she asked therefore.

"Don't mind him," said Ma with a throwaway gesture of the hand.

"I'm Jeff Morrison," said the newcomer. "I am a doctor and—"

"Will you just look inside!" Ma yelled, and gesticulated wildly in the direction of Odelia's house.

Marge glanced up at the place, and when she didn't see any smoke or flames emanating from the structure, already breathed a little easier. "What's wrong?" she asked.

"Just look for yourself," said Ma, crossing her arms in front of her chest. "You'll find out soon enough what's wrong." And as Marge set foot for the kitchen door, Ma added, "And I blame the cats!"

The moment she opened the kitchen door, she was almost attacked by a swarm of birds that seemed to be everywhere! The kitchen was filled with them, and so was the living room. "My God!" she yelled as birds got into her hair and flew against her face. "Who let these in!"

As quickly as she had entered, she was outside again, opening the door for good measure so the birds could take off. But oddly enough, none of them did. They just stayed put.

"What's going on?" she asked as she touched her hair to make sure no birds were stuck in there.

"Dooley extended an invitation to one bird," Ma explained. "One bird!" she said, holding up a single digit. "And of course, this bird had to take advantage of Dooley's hospitality and invite his entire family to come and stay. Hundreds of birds, Marge, possibly thousands!"

"Who is Dooley?" asked the stranger, but Marge decided to ignore him for the moment, as did Ma.

"We have to uninvite them," she said. "They're going to poop all over the place and make a right mess."

"And we have to do it before Odelia gets here," said Ma. "Otherwise, she'll fly off the handle. You know how stressed out she has been lately, with all the work she has on her plate, not to mention four cats, a husband, and a baby she needs to wrangle. It's too much for any human being, and adding

Hitchcock's birds to the mix is going to send her over the edge."

"They're not budging," said Marge.

"I told you: Dooley invited them and now they're here to stay."

"So, this Dooley would be…" the stranger tried again, but once again both Marge and her mother decided to ignore him.

"Where are the cats?" she asked.

"Good question," said Ma. "Where are the cats? I've been asking myself that very same question. Looks like they invited the birds in and then took off—probably knowing there would be hell to pay."

"We need Dooley to retract his invitation," said Marge.

"So Dooley is your daughter's husband?" asked the stranger.

This time Marge turned to face him. "I'm sorry, but who are you?"

"Like I said, I'm Jeff Morrison. I'm a doctor and your mother gave me a lift. My car broke down, you see, so I had to hitchhike my way here and—"

"Jeff is a brain surgeon," Ma explained.

"Is that a fact?"

"So Dooley is your daughter's husband?" asked the brain surgeon. "And he let the birds into the house?"

"No, Dooley is my…" Almost Marge had said Dooley was her cat, but that wouldn't do, as outsiders didn't need to know that she and her mother could talk to their cats, and so could Odelia and Odelia's daughter Grace.

"Dooley is a friend of the family," Ma said, giving Marge a wink. "Though we're a little upset with him right now, aren't we, Marge?"

"We certainly are," Marge confirmed.

Just then, there was a noise near the hedge, and when

they all looked over, Marge saw that Kurt was trying to attract their attention. "So how is Dooley?" he asked.

"Dooley is fine," said Ma snappishly. "Though I can't guarantee he will be fine for much longer. He let a horde of birds into the house and we can't get them to leave."

"Oh, that's too bad," said Kurt, who Marge had never known to be particularly concerned with their cats before. Then again, the man was getting older, and people do tend to mellow with age—at least some of them do. "I saved him from a tree this morning, you see," Odelia's neighbor explained. "He was stuck up there and so I got him down. I borrowed Tex's ladder from the garden house, Marge. I hope you don't mind."

"No, I don't," said Marge. "That was very thoughtful of you, Kurt."

"So... Dooley was stuck in a tree?" asked Ma's brain surgeon.

"Yeah, the poor fella was crying piteously, and so Gilda figured we probably needed to save him as he couldn't get down on his own."

Marge now noticed that Gilda had joined her boyfriend at the fence and understood all. Even though Kurt wasn't a cat person—quite the opposite, in fact—Gilda was. So Gilda had probably pressured her boyfriend into saving Dooley from his predicament.

"Thanks, Gilda," she said warmly.

"Oh, that's all right," said Gilda. "You would do the same for Fifi if she got stuck in a tree, wouldn't you?"

"Fifi would never get stuck in a tree," Kurt argued. "She's much too clever for that."

Ma narrowed her eyes at their neighbor. "Are you implying that Dooley isn't as clever as Fifi, Kurt Mayfield?"

"Oh, no, absolutely not!" Kurt hastened to say. "Just that dogs... don't climb trees... like cats do."

"What cat would this be?" asked Jeff Morrison, very confused at this point.

"Dooley," said Kurt curtly. "And when I saw that even Max couldn't save him, I figured I needed to do something. He could have been stuck up there for the rest of the day, or maybe jumped down and injured himself."

"It's fine," said Ma, as she darted a nervous glance at Jeff. For some reason, she seemed determined to make a good impression on the man, which surprised Marge, as her mother never tried to make a good impression on anyone— quite the contrary, in fact. "Thanks, Kurt."

"What's with all the birds?" asked Gilda, having noticed that Odelia's house was filled to capacity with the feathered little creatures.

"Dooley invited them in. Can you believe it? And of course the one bird had to go and bring along all of his friends and relatives. And now we can't get rid of them!" She frowned at Marge, who had given her leg a vicious kick. Then Ma seemed to realize her faux-pas, and smiled sweetly. "I mean, Dooley accidentally left the pet flap open and the birds got in. Silly cat."

"He must have felt traumatized from being up in that tree," said Gilda. "Poor thing. And now you have those birds to contend with. If you want, Kurt will take care of them— won't you, Kurt?"

"What? What do you mean?" asked Kurt, not happy at being pushed to do something he didn't enjoy for the second time that day. But when Gilda gave him a penetrating look, he quickly relented. "Okay, fine. But how do you suggest we get them out of there?"

"You'll figure it out," said Gilda.

"Maybe you can play something on one of your instruments," Ma suggested. "You are a music man, aren't you?"

"I'm a retired music teacher," said Kurt huffily. "Not a music man."

"But you play an instrument, don't you? The flute maybe? Birds like flutes, don't they? So play your flute and maybe they will come out and sit on your shoulders. Like the Pied Piper. Do you know that story?"

Kurt didn't seem pleased to be compared to the Pied Piper, for he gave Ma a dirty look. "Yes, I know the story of the Pied Piper, but I don't think—"

"Go and get your flute, Kurt," said Gilda as she rubbed his arm. She turned to Marge. "He's such a great musician. But so used to hiding his light under a bushel that I can never get him to perform in front of other people."

"You should join a band," said Ma. "Or an orchestra."

"I'm not good enough for that," said Kurt, and for the first time since they had made the man's acquaintance, he was actually blushing.

"Nonsense," said Gilda. "You're aces, and you know it. Just play the flute for us, Kurt. Do it now," she added, and her words brooked no contest.

And so Kurt hurried into the house to fetch his flute.

"You'll see. He's really good," said Gilda.

"Are you sure the birds will respond to the sound of the flute?" asked Marge, who had never heard of such a thing.

"Oh, absolutely," said Gilda. "But only if it's being played by an amazing and talented musician, like Kurt."

"They'll go and sit around Kurt and listen to him," said Ma. "Just like in Mary Poppins when the doves flock to the bird woman." She frowned. "Though I don't remember her playing the flute. Might have been a violin."

"So… Dooley is a cat?" asked Jeff, proving that he was no fool.

Marge and her mother shared a look, and Marge turned

to the man and took him by the shoulder. "You misheard. Like Ma said, Dooley is a friend of the family."

"Oh, I see," said the surgeon, but it was obvious that he didn't.

"Let me show you the house," said Ma, and hooked her arm through his.

"Show him the house?" asked Marge. "Why do you want to show him the house?"

But her mother was already leading the guy away. Somehow Marge got the impression that her life had just gotten a whole lot more complicated.

CHAPTER 8

Theo and Taylor had raced back to the van, and Theo had managed to get a fresh pair of pants to replace the ones that the dog had chewed up. Feeling refreshed and happy to get rid of that mutt, they decided to continue their job for the day: scamming credulous people out of their money. It wasn't hard, and they had been doing it successfully for quite a while. "Let's try the house next door," Taylor now suggested.

"Are you nuts?" asked Theo. "What if that dog returns and tries to take another bite out of me?"

"I like to keep things organized," Taylor argued. "If we skip a house now, we might never get back to it."

"Just make a note."

"I don't want to make a note, all right? I want to keep this organized. And the organized way of doing things is to do the next house. And that would be… Harrington Street 43," said Taylor, who had always been a pain in the ass, Theo now realized.

"I think you've got OCD," he said.

"I don't have OCD," said Taylor. "I'm just organized, that's all. What's the matter with being organized? It's the road to success."

"Says you."

"No, says everybody."

"Name me one person who thinks that going back to the place where a dog just tried to emasculate me is the road to success?"

"We're not going back to that place. We're going next door."

"Oh, God," said Theo, throwing up his hands. He took a sip from his flask of coffee and replaced it on the dash. "Okay, fine," he said finally. "Let's take the next house. But if that dog tries to take another bite of me, I'm blaming you."

"You won't have to blame me, because it's not going to happen," said Taylor, glad that he had won this argument.

Both crooks got out of the van and set foot for Harrington Street 43.

"Let's go for the gnomes spiel," said Taylor.

"Why?"

"Because I'm up to date on it, that's why."

"It doesn't matter if it's gnomes or something else, is it?"

"But I like the gnomes," argued Taylor.

"God, you really are OCD," said Theo.

"I just happen to like gnomes, all right? What's wrong with that?"

"Nothing," said Theo, rolling his eyes.

"I saw that."

"If course you did."

They had arrived at the house in question, and as luck would have it, quite a number of gnomes stood in attendance in the front yard.

"I think we're in luck," said Theo.

"I *know* we're in luck," said Taylor. "We saw the gnomes from the Trapper backyard."

"So that's why you wanted to come here!"

"Will you lower your voice? And get in character," Taylor admonished him.

And so Theo straightened. "*Think* like an IRS agent. *Be* the IRS agent. *Feel* like an IRS agent," he murmured. If method actors could do it, they could do it. They were, after all, method crooks, as Taylor never stopped pointing out, ad nauseam.

"I have this whole script written out, you know," said Taylor. "I sent it to you, remember? Did you even read it?"

"Of course I read your script."

"No, you didn't. What section of the tax code deals with the gnome tax?"

"There *is* no gnome tax!"

Taylor gave him a stern-faced look.

"All right. There is a gnome tax. Of course there is a gnome tax."

"We're method crooks, Theo. *Think* gnome tax. *Be* the gnome tax."

"OCD," he sang quietly.

"How many times do I have to say it? I'm not OCD!"

Just then the door was yanked open and an old lady appeared. Immediately, Theo felt his mood lift. Old people were easy marks. The older they were, the easier to scam. "My dear lady," he said before he felt a kick in the backside from his colleague and remembered he was an IRS agent and not a priest—one of their other scams. "I mean, Mrs…"

"Poole?" Taylor prompted.

"What do you want?" the old lady asked, giving them a look that didn't exactly inspire confidence in their scheme.

"I have noticed that you have several gnomes in your

front yard," said Theo. "And as you may or may not know, the governor of the great State of New York, in his eternal wisdom, has recently introduced a gnome tax."

"And unfortunately, according to our information, you haven't paid your annual gnome tax," said Taylor. The man might have OCD and be a pain in the ass sometimes, but the two of them formed a well-oiled team, which is what made them one of the most successful double criminal acts in the state.

"I don't know nothing about that," said the woman, and slammed the door in their faces in a surprising display of force. Luckily for Theo, he had reinforced his shoe with solid steel, so when he put the tip between the door before it closed he didn't feel a thing.

"I don't know if you're aware that there are severe penalties involved, Mrs. Poole," he said. "According to section eight of the…"

"Oh, buzz off, bozo," said the woman, giving him a poke in the eye that made the so-called IRS agent take a step backward, enabling the old lady to slam the door shut, this time successfully.

"She poked me in the eye!" Theo cried. "She actually went and poked me in the eye!"

"According to section ten of the tax code, poking an IRS agent in the eye is a punishable offense," said Taylor sternly.

"Who cares!" he said viciously. His eye was seriously hurting, and coming after the incident with the dog, his mood was plummeting fast once again. "Let's go next door," he suggested therefore.

"But we aren't finished here yet," Taylor pointed out.

"And I say we are," he said, his eye smarting something terrible. And before Taylor had a chance to protest, he stomped off. Whatever his colleague said, he wasn't going to be subjected to more abuse from that horrible woman. "Easy target, my foot," he muttered as he took up position next door to the Pooles. According to his information, at this address a reporter lived, and he hoped she wouldn't be home so they could scratch this address off their list as well. The further he got away from that dog, the better.

He pressed his finger to the buzzer, and when nothing happened, pressed it again.

Suddenly the door was opened, and he found himself staring into the face of a middle-aged lady. Behind her, he saw dozens of birds flitting hither and thither. He gaped at the birds, his jaw dropping a couple of inches in the process.

"Yes?" said the woman. "What is it? I'm a little busy here," she added in an apologetic tone.

Lucky for him, Taylor had joined him and took out his badge and introduced himself.

"The IRS?" asked the lady.

"Yes, Mrs. Kingsley," said Taylor. "We're IRS agents, and it has come to our attention that you haven't paid your taxes."

"What taxes? I always pay my taxes."

A clever look had stolen over Taylor's face as he pointed to the birds. "You haven't paid your bird tax."

Genius, Theo thought. Even though his partner was a pain in the patootie sometimes, you had to hand it to him: the guy was a criminal mastermind. Bird tax! He would never have thought of that in a million years!

"Bird tax? What bird tax?" asked the woman.

"The governor of our fine state, in his infinite wisdom, has decided to introduce a bird tax," said Taylor. "And according to our information, you haven't paid your bird tax this year. There is a penalty involved, I'm afraid, and an interest for every day that you're late with your payment."

"The tax is calculated by the number of birds you have," said Theo as he licked his lips and took in the sheer number of birds. There were dozens—maybe hundreds of the creatures! If he wasn't mistaken, they had just hit the jackpot!

"I don't know anything about that," said the woman, who seemed a little distracted, Theo thought. "And besides, this isn't my house. My daughter lives here. I live next door," she explained. "Also, these birds aren't hers. They accidentally got in, and we're trying to get rid of them."

"Be that as it may, the birds are on the premises, so the taxes owed will have to be paid," said Taylor smoothly, like the professional method criminal that he was. "We'll count the birds now. Or maybe we can make some kind of deal?"

"A lump sum," said Theo, "Payable immediately."

"In cash," said Taylor. "Unless you want to pay the full amount with penalties and interest, which are levied at one hundred percent of the original sum."

"Look, you'll have to come back some other time," said the woman. "My daughter isn't home right now, and neither is her husband, so..."

"I'm afraid the longer you wait, the higher the interest," said Taylor.

"Best to pay now," said Theo. "Before we have to come back with a debt collector and take possession of your furniture. Your television, your stereo, your phone..."

The woman looked rattled, Theo saw, and he knew they had her. They had done this long enough to be able to read their targets like a book. And they would have gone for the jugular if not for the man who suddenly appeared behind the lady. He was tall and big and looked like a bodybuilder.

"What's going on here?" asked the guy.

"Can you deal with this, Chase?" asked the woman. "These gentlemen are from the IRS, and they're here to collect on a bird tax."

"There is no bird tax," said the man calmly.

Theo drew himself up to his full height. "I'll have you know that according to section four of the tax code—"

"And I'll have you know that according to section five of the penal code, it's illegal to impersonate an IRS agent and try and scam people," said the guy. And then he fastened his hands on him and Taylor's necks and said, "Detective Chase Kingsley. Hampton Cove PD. You're both under arrest."

CHAPTER 9

Hannah Dunlop closed her curtains and shook her head. "There's something going on across the street at the Pooles," she said.

"Something is always going on with the Pooles," said her husband without looking up from his newspaper.

"Yes, but this time it looks serious. That big lug of a policeman just arrested two men who look like Jehovah's Witnesses or Mormons or both. I think the Pooles may have just gotten in way over their heads. You can't go and arrest the Lord's messengers."

"Is it those same fools who dropped by the house a couple of days ago? If so, Kingsley is right to arrest them," said her husband as he turned the page.

"And why is that?"

"Because they weren't Jehovah's Witnesses at all but so-called IRS agents. Couple of scammers, if you ask me. They took one look at the wall and tried to make me believe that the governor had introduced a painting tax last year and that we hadn't paid it. I told them I'd take my chances and kicked them out."

"Let's hope you were right and they weren't a pair of actual IRS agents," said Hannah as she took a seat in the armchair next to her husband. "Otherwise we're in big trouble. Those tax people are nothing to be trifled with. They always get their man."

"I think you'll find that's the Canadian Mounties," he said.

That was the problem with Norbert, she thought. He always had an answer for everything. Too bad they had been married for so long she couldn't divorce the guy. It just wasn't worth it after all those years. And besides, her family would kill her if she did. With five kids, ten grandkids, and seventeen great-grandkids, the scandal would rock the family and would create a lot of fuss that she didn't need.

She eyed him closely and wondered if he had another liver spot on the side of his head. He had never been a handsome man, but he had not aged well. Even though he was only seventy-two, which wasn't all that old, he looked a decade older. She should have listened to her sister Holly, who had warned her against marrying the guy. But then he'd had the gift of the gab and had been such a smooth talker—and such a wonderful dancer—that she had fallen for him hook, line, and sinker.

It had taken her a couple of years before she discovered she had made a terrible mistake when he had dropped all the pretense and had shown his true colors by giving her a couple of smacks across the head when she didn't serve his food fast enough. Another smack when she ruined his best shirt in the wash. And another when he thought she was flirting with the mailman. By then they had four kids with a fifth one on the way, and she couldn't be bothered getting rid of the guy. Besides, her family was crazy about him—except her sisters. Sometimes she thought they loved him more than they did her. Especially Dad, who thought the sun shone out of Norbert's behind and would have killed her if she even mentioned the D word in connection with the guy.

Over the years things had gotten a lot easier. He had mostly stopped hitting her when he had stopped being attracted to her, so that was something. He had also started chasing other women and having affairs, so that took care of another problem she'd had. And now they simply tolerated one another, like the old couple that they were.

"Francis Reilly is dropping by later on," she now told him.

No response.

"He wants to talk about some church business."

"Probably needs more money for the church roof," he said. "Francis always needs more money for that darn roof. Same story for thirty years."

"Yeah, well, he's dropping by so we'll be in the kitchen."

"Fine with me," he said and turned a page. "Just don't give him any money. That roof is just fine, and I should know, because I put it up there."

That, he had. And he'd done such a shoddy job that half the tiles had blown off during a storm, and Francis had to bring in a different roofer to redo the work. But then Norbert had always been something of a hustler: a gifted roofer, but he couldn't be bothered. Too busy chasing skirts and drinking with his buddies to do a proper job. Which is why his company was glad to be rid of him when he put in for early retirement. Too bad for her, since she now had to put up with him even more than before.

The doorbell rang, and she opened the door. The priest hurried in, looking over his shoulder. "Quick," he said. "I don't want to be seen."

"Seen by whom?" she asked, wondering what was going on.

"Someone was following me on the street just now," he said, and sounded out of breath.

"Someone was following you? But who? And why?"

"I'm not sure," he said. "I thought it might have been a mugger, but I didn't want to look over my shoulder too much. He followed me all the way from St. John's to Harrington Street. I did a couple of detours, and he was behind me every step of the way. But I think I finally managed to shake him off three blocks from here." He glanced out of the window, making sure not to touch the curtain. "There! That's him!"

Norbert, even though he was not a big fan of the priest, was intrigued. He joined them at the window. "I know that guy," he now declared.

"You do?" asked Francis.

"Sure. That's Benny Dowd. He was in the paper. Murder one. Killed three men without batting an eye, then dissolved them in his bathtub."

"Dissolved them?" asked Hannah. "How do you dissolve a person?"

"In acid," said Norbert acidly as he grabbed for his paper.

The priest's face softened. "Oh, but I know Benny. He's a parishioner."

Norbert rolled his eyes. "And why am I not surprised?" He returned to his armchair. "Don't tell me. Part of that rehabilitation scheme of yours?"

"That's right," said Francis. "Benny is in my rehabilitation program. So that's why he was following me. He's very shy, you know. Probably wants to talk to me but was afraid to approach. I'll talk to him later. But first…" He gave Hannah a meaningful look, and they both retreated into the kitchen.

As she poured the good father a cup of her best coffee, and offered him a piece of her homemade cake, he gave her a grateful smile. "This is so wonderful of you," he said. "You really shouldn't have, Hannah."

"But I want to," she said. Apart from her two sisters,

Francis Reilly might be the only friend in the world she had, and she liked to spoil him. After she had served him an extra-large slice of her red velvet cake, she took a seat across the kitchen table and watched him expectantly. The man of God closed his eyes as he savored the treat.

"Truly divine," he said. "You are without a doubt the most gifted baker I know, Hannah Dunlop."

"Oh, you're just saying that."

"No, I mean it. And that's exactly what I wanted to talk to you about."

"My cake?" She didn't know why, but she felt a sense of disappointment. On the phone, he had told her that he had something very important to ask her. But if it was to ask her if she could bake a cake for the annual church raffle, he could have spared himself the trip and asked her on the phone.

"Well, yes," he admitted. "The church roof is leaking again, as I may have mentioned to you."

He had only mentioned it about a dozen times already, and even though she hated to admit that Norbert was right, the simple fact was that he was right.

"The thing is that we need to collect an additional twenty thousand, and your red velvet cake has always proven extremely popular, so if I could appeal to your sense of community and your Christian spirit once again…"

"Of course," she assured him. "How many do you need?"

"Well…" He thought for a moment. "Considering that your cakes sell like hot cakes." He laughed at his own joke for a moment before turning serious again. "How about two hundred?" When her face clouded, he quickly said, "That's too much. Of course it is too much."

"No, it's fine." She could already imagine how she would be in her kitchen for days to bake that number of cakes, and wondered not for the first time why he couldn't simply ask one of his baker parishioners to do the honors. They had the equipment to handle such a large volume. "I'll just ask my sister Holly to pitch in." And maybe her sister Lee as well. Between the three of them, they might manage.

"Let's leave it for now," he said, making a gesture of the hand. "Two hundred is a lot. Maybe half of that would be more manageable."

"No, I'll do it," she said. "Two hundred cakes coming right up." She gave him a brave smile. And could already imagine Norbert's words when she told him that Francis wanted her to bake no less than two hundred cakes for the church raffle. He'd laugh his ass off and tell her she was a chump. And then he'd accuse her of being in love with Francis and laugh some more.

The rest of the conversation mainly consisted of small talk and some mild and innocent gossip about some of the other members of the church raffle commission. When finally Francis had eaten his second piece of cake and drunk his second cup of coffee, he got up to leave.

"And how are things with Norbert now?" he asked with a look of concern on his face. He was one of the only people she had ever confided in about the abuse she had suffered in the early years of her marriage.

"It's okay," she assured him. "He does his things and I do mine, and never our paths cross. Which is exactly how it should be."

"No, it's not," he said. "You deserve happiness, Hannah. Not this…" He gestured vaguely in the direction of the living room. "This monster who has made it his mission in life to make you feel miserable."

"I'm not going to divorce Norbert, Francis," she told him not for the first time. They'd had this conversation before, and she had told him exactly what she had told Holly and Lee: she was too old to divorce and live all by herself. If there was one thing she hated more than having to live with that no-good husband of hers, it was being alone. At least Norbert took care of a lot of the stuff she couldn't. Like driving everywhere, the financial stuff, taxes, fixing things around the house. The list was endless, and just the thought of having to do all of that by herself made her feel nauseous.

"Think about it," he said as he placed a hand on her shoulder.

Just at that moment, Norbert walked in, and when he saw the intimate scene, a slight grin momentarily slid up his face. "Looks like that guy is back, Francis."

"What guy?" asked the priest.

"Your serial killer friend."

Francis smiled. "That's all in the past."

"So he found God, huh? Is that what you're saying?"

"That's exactly right, Norbert." He gave the man a penetrating look. "And it's not too late for you, you know."

"Oh, get lost, you old fool," said Norbert viciously, causing Hannah to look at her husband in shock. You didn't say that kind of thing to a man of God!

But clearly Norbert couldn't care less, for he had already retreated back to the living room, leaving Hannah to see the priest out, but not before profusely apologizing for the terrible and inexcusable behavior of her husband.

CHAPTER 10

While we had gone for a little tour around the block to have a think about how we were going to get rid of those unwelcome feathered house guests, our humans had arrived home, and when we returned, we found Vesta accosting a man in the middle of the street, accusing him of being a crook and carrying out a citizen's arrest.

The man seemed almost embarrassed for being arrested by a senior citizen and tried to assure her that he wasn't a crook at all but simply a man looking for salvation.

"So you're trying to tell me that you were chasing Francis Reilly because you're having trouble with your soul, is that it?" she asked. She had planted her hands on her hips and was watching him closely, just in case he tried to do a runner.

Father Reilly had joined her and seemed almost embarrassed. "I know this man, Vesta," he assured her. "He's one of my parishioners. Isn't that right, Benny?"

"All I wanted was to have a chat with you, Father," the latter said now. "Ever since I came for confession the other day, I've been thinking about the things you told me, and so I wanted to talk to you some more. Face to face, as it were."

The priest opened his arms wide in a gesture of forgiveness. "And here I thought that you were trying to mug me!" he said, smiling widely.

"I still think he was trying to mug you," said Gran, who isn't the kind of person who takes a person at his word.

"I promise I wasn't," said Benny. "The thing is that I'm trying to come clean about my sins, and Father Reilly is the first person who has helped me see things more clearly."

"I'm so glad our conversation proved beneficial," said the priest, clapping the man on the back. "Now tell me, son, how I can be of service to you?"

"Are you sure about this, Francis?" asked Gran.

"Absolutely," said the priest, and started off along the street with the man in tow. Looked like they had a lot of things to talk about.

Gran shook her head as she watched the twosome take off. "Francis has always been too gullible for his own good. But what can you do?" She then cast a baleful eye at us. "I have a bone to pick with the four of you."

"A bone to pick?" asked Dooley nervously.

"Picking bones is more a dog's game, isn't it, Gran?" asked Brutus, trying to laugh off her question.

But Gran wasn't in the mood for jokes. "Inside," she said. "Before the neighbors think I've gone crazy."

I could have told her they already thought she was crazy, but somehow I didn't think that would sit well with her, especially considering the foul mood she seemed to be in.

We hurried after her into the Poole home, and the moment the door was closed, she stood before us, tapping her foot impatiently. "Well? I'm waiting."

"Is this about the birds?" I ventured, figuring we might as well get it over with.

"How did you guess! Please tell me you have an idea how to get rid of them."

We all looked at Dooley, who shrank a little. "I'm sorry, Gran," he said in a small voice.

"You should never have invited those birds to come and stay with us," said Gran. "Now we'll never get rid of these creatures."

"In Dooley's defense," I said, "he only invited the one bird. The rest were invited by that bird."

"I know he only invited the one bird, Max. But that's no excuse."

"Stewart," Brutus clarified. "He said he was an orphan and that he didn't have a place to stay, and so Dooley said he could stay with us."

"He fooled you, didn't he?" said Gran. "Birds don't need a place to stay! The world is their oyster. They're not like cats. They always have food wherever they go, and they live in trees and under gutters and anywhere else they manage to make a home for themselves."

"I didn't think," said Dooley. "I'm sorry, Gran. So what are you going to do now?"

"We have to get rid of them somehow," said Gran. "Kurt is going to blow his whistle, but I'm not so sure if that will do the trick."

"Kurt will blow his whistle?" I asked, figuring she was cracking a joke.

"Yeah, Gilda's idea," said Gran. "In fact, we better go over there and see how things are going. If my hunch is correct, this whole whistle business will backfire dramatically." And as she led us out of the house again, then around the back to the backyard, she explained, "Marge and I wanted to get those birds out of there before Odelia found out, but in the meantime, Chase arrived home, so that didn't work. Though if we can get them out before she sees the mess that those birds created, maybe everything will be fine."

"We'll help clean up the mess, Gran," Dooley promised.

"Too right you will help clean up the mess. After all, if you hadn't let them into the house, this wouldn't have happened in the first place."

We had arrived in our own backyard, and the scene that met our eyes was something to behold: Kurt Mayfield stood there, blowing on a flute, with Gilda watching on, a look of admiration on her face. Of Chase, there was no trace, but then I figured he was inside, trying to catch those birds.

Who was there was Marge, and she didn't look happy.

"So is it working?" asked Gran as she joined her daughter.

"So far, nothing," said Marge.

"Where is Chase?"

"Oh, he arrested a couple of crooks," said Marge, as if this was a common thing. Which I guess it probably was, since Chase is a cop, and arresting criminals is in the job description.

"Crooks?"

"Two guys impersonating a pair of IRS agents and trying to impose a fine on me for not paying my 'bird tax.'"

"Probably the same guys who tried to impose a gnome tax on me," said Gran. "I kicked them out."

"I probably should have kicked them out," said Marge. "But with those birds, I kinda got distracted. Good thing Chase showed up and read them the riot act—and their rights."

Meanwhile, Kurt kept on blowing his flute, and even though it sounded pretty great, I have to say, from inside the house, nothing was happening.

"No birds," Marge determined.

"I guess they don't like Kurt's playing," said Gran.

"Or maybe they like it, but they like staying at the house

more."

"I guess so."

It was at this moment that Harriet stepped to the fore, followed by Brutus, and assumed a position next to Kurt. The retired music teacher, without stopping his performance, darted a curious look at the cats, then at his girlfriend. Gilda shrugged.

And as Harriet opened her mouth, and also Brutus, both cats burst into song. I think the idea was to accompany the flute playing with some vocal accompaniment. Unfortunately, neither Harriet nor Brutus are gifted *chanteurs*, and as their singing scratched my eardrums and those of all present, I could see from the painful grimace that spread across the faces of our humans that even though the intention behind their initiative had been noble and praiseworthy, the execution left something to be desired.

The end result was that Kurt had to stop playing the flute so he could cover his ears with his hands. After all, humans only have two hands, and he needed both to make sure his ears didn't start bleeding. Before long, both he and Gilda had retreated to their own home, and even Marge and Gran, who were used to Harriet's caterwauling, seemed to have a hard time stomaching her endeavors.

"Where are the birds, Max?" asked Dooley.

"Inside, I guess," I said. "Taking cover."

If I was a bird, and I heard Harriet and Brutus sing, I wouldn't venture outside either. Which gave me a bright idea.

And so I applauded heartily before joining my friends. "That was wonderful," I told them. "Absolutely amazing. But I don't think the birds can hear you. Why don't you take this impromptu concert inside? I think they'll be much more appreciative of your efforts to lighten up their day."

Harriet gave me a warm smile. "Spoken like a true music

lover, Max. Of course we will go inside."

And so she and Brutus headed in through the pet flap. Moments later, the duo recommenced their musical interlude. And this time it wasn't long before a steady stream of birds literally flew from the house. Out they came, dozens at a time, and all of them looking extremely perturbed, not to say traumatized, by the auditory experience they had just gone through. Knowing that birds have very sensitive ears—much better than humans' ears—I guess they couldn't take this assault on their fine sense of hearing.

The last one to vacate the premises was Stewart. He gave me a pained look. "You never told me that this was part of the setup, Max," he said.

"What can I say?" I said. "Harriet just loves to sing."

"Does she do this often?" he asked.

"Every hour, on the hour," I said.

"God have mercy," he said, and flitted off, possibly to find some other numpkin to use his orphan sob story on.

"You can stop now!" I bellowed for the benefit of Harriet and Brutus. But of course they couldn't hear me. Or maybe they were so engrossed in their artistic endeavor that they didn't want to stop. That's the problem with these artistic types: they will go on and on until they run out of steam—which can take a long time.

"Maybe it's a good thing, Max," said Dooley. "There may be stragglers that are hard to shift. This will flush them all out."

I gave him a smile. "Well put, Dooley."

Looked like we had solved the bird problem. And just in time, too, for just then, Odelia came around the corner, carrying Grace on her arm. She gave us a smile and entered. And as Dooley and I shared a look, it wasn't even ten seconds before a loud scream sounded from inside.

I guess Odelia had discovered the state of the house.

CHAPTER 11

It had taken the concerted efforts of the entire family to make the house look more or less presentable again. When Odelia had entered the place, she had been shocked at how terrible a state it was in, and what those birds had done with the place. When she asked her cats how the birds had gained access to the place in the first place, their answers weren't exactly satisfactory, which made her suspect that they probably were to blame somehow, but then they had also been instrumental in getting the birds out of the house, so she figured she shouldn't be too hard on them.

Especially Harriet and Brutus had done their utmost to get the birds away from there, and to make them stop destroying the house.

"I never knew how much of a mess birds could make," said Mom as she looked up from her efforts to clean the floor. She wiped her sweaty brow. "Now I understand why you never wanted to keep birds, honey."

"I never wanted to keep birds because I believe that birds shouldn't be kept in a cage," said Odelia. Though now that she saw what a mess they made, she seriously thought she should probably amend her philosophy and add a second item to the list: they shouldn't live in cages, but they also shouldn't live in the house, on account of the fact that they had no sense of hygiene.

"Is that poop or by design?" asked Gran as she studied a spot on the wall right next to the kitchen counter.

"By design, more or less," said Odelia. "Grace spat out a piece of Froot Loop, and it stuck to the wall, and since I forgot to wipe it, it stayed stuck."

"I'll get it off," said Gran and applied her nails to dislodge the thing.

"Good thing that Kurt was here to try and lure them away," said Gran as she stuck her tongue between her lips and really went to town on that Froot Loop.

"Kurt was here? He got rid of the birds?"

"Well, no," said Mom. "He tried to get rid of the birds by playing on his flute." When her daughter gave her a look of incredulity, she said, "It wasn't my idea, honey. It was Gilda's. She figured that Kurt's playing might attract the birds, on account of how beautiful they would think it was. The Pied Piper principle. Only problem was that her theory had never been tested in the field, and it failed to make any impression on the birds, I'm afraid."

"Harriet's singing did the trick," said Gran. "So there was something in Gilda's theory about music having an impact on birds. Only not in the way she anticipated. More law of repulsion, less law of attraction, if you catch my drift."

Grace, who was trying to help them out, had scooped up a piece of bird poop from the coffee table and now held it out to her mother.

"Don't touch that, honey," she said. "Where are your gloves?" She had doled out gloves for all the different members of her team, but apparently, some of them had already gone missing.

"So I'm going on a double date soon," said Gran.

"Oh, with that nice doctor you met?" asked Mom.

"Well, not him, unfortunately. Though he does seem really nice, doesn't he? No, he's going to set me and Scarlett up with a couple of colleagues of his. So very soon now I might be getting married again. To a doctor!"

Odelia exchanged a look with her mother. The last thing they needed was another marriage taking place in the family, and most definitely not Gran's, who had a habit of making a mess of anything she did, even more so than those birds, who, after all, couldn't help themselves. Gran could help herself, but she still created more trouble than she was worth.

"So I've put him up in the spare bedroom," said Gran now.

Mom looked up. "Hm?"

"I put Jeff in the spare bedroom. I would have given him my room, but it's such a drag having to rearrange everything, and besides, I don't think it's proper for a man to sleep in a girl's bedroom."

"You've… set Jeff up in the spare bedroom? But why?"

"Well, he is staying with us," Gran clarified. "Didn't I tell you?"

"No," said Mom after a pause. "No, you didn't."

"I guess I must have forgotten. Well, he's staying with us, and I gotta tell you, he was really looking forward to exchanging his views on the medical profession with Tex."

Odelia could tell that Mom didn't agree with her mother inviting people to stay with them out of the blue, and without consulting her. Then again, it could have been worse. Jeff sounded like a good sort of person. And also, he was a doctor, and it was true that Dad would enjoy exchanging views with the man. So maybe it wasn't such a bad thing.

"Okay, I think this part is clean," she said. She hoped the birds hadn't gotten upstairs and into the bedrooms. Otherwise, they'd be busy all night cleaning everything. Even now she didn't think they'd get through doing the entire thing in one evening. They might have to get back to it tomorrow, but hopefully by then they'd have everything nice and clean again.

"Let's lock the pet flap for now," Mom suggested. "Just in case those birds decide to come back, I mean."

"The cats won't like it," said Odelia. "They love being able to come and go." Not to mention that she also loved the convenience of that flap. Their cats liked to go to the park at night, to attend cat choir, and if she had to open and close the door every time they wanted to come in or leave, she'd go nuts, since that's all they did.

"I don't think those birds can come in through the pet flap," said Gran. "It's too hard to flit to and fro by lifting that heavy flap. Birds are delicate creatures, after all. Not a lot of muscle mass packed on those tiny frames."

"So how did they get in here in the first place?" asked Mom.

"Odelia must have left the door open again, as usual," Gran suggested.

"I did not leave the door open," said Odelia, with an incredulous laugh. "And what's so usual about it? I never leave the door open, and neither does Grace."

"Just saying," said Gran with a shrug, "someone must have let the birds in. Otherwise, how come there were hundreds of them flapping around?"

"They must have entered through the pet flap," said Mom, sticking to her theory. "Which is why we should lock it for a couple of days. Until they give up. Birds are creatures of habit, so when they discover they can't get in, they'll find some other home they can terrorize with their presence."

It certainly was a thought Odelia needed to take on board. And as she put the finishing touches to the kitchen counter—which had taken quite a lot of effort to look spanking clean again—her husband walked in.

"Those two won't be going anywhere for the time being," he said with a look of satisfaction on his face.

"Who?" she asked.

"Oh, haven't you heard?" asked Gran. "We caught two crooks trying to swindle us."

"They were trying to make me believe that they were IRS agents looking to collect on the bird tax," said Mom. "If you can believe it."

"Bird tax? What is the bird tax?"

"There is no bird tax!" said Gran. "It was just a scam. They tried to make me pay the gnome tax, on account of the gnomes that your dad collects."

"They're locked up for the night," Chase assured them. "So they won't be collecting any more tax for a while. And if the judge isn't too lenient at the arraignment they might actually do some hard time this time."

"Why, have they been at it before?" asked Mom.

"Sure have," said Chase as he inspected the floor and discovered he had to step lightly if he wanted to avoid stepping into some of that bird poop. "Plenty of convictions on their criminal records. A pair of career criminals if ever I've seen them. Been pulling this kind of stunt many times, with small variations on the same theme. Last time they were doing the rounds they were pretending to be nurses, and while one of them treated the patient, the other one went searching for the person's valuables. Mostly they scammed older folks that way, though now they seem to have expanded their scope and are targeting the general population." He frowned. "The birds really went to town on our living room. How did they get in in the first place?"

"The cats invited one bird in, and that one bird invited the rest of his family," said Mom. "The upshot is that we've been trying to make everything look spic and span again."

"Well, good luck with that," he said and turned to his favorite sofa to take a seat. Unfortunately for him, the sofa hadn't been cleaned yet, and there was no place to sit.

"Better give us a helping hand, Chase," said Mom, who didn't like it when the menfolk treated the womenfolk as unpaid labor. She handed him a bucket and a wet rag. "Start with that couch and work your way around the television nook, will you?"

It was a credit to the husband Odelia had married that the cop took the bucket and the rag without a second thought and immediately started cleaning the couch. The time when women were in charge of the house while the men worked at the office was long gone, and a good thing, too. She didn't think she could be married to a man who came home, dropped down on the couch, and expected her to bring him his slippers, his cigar, and his newspaper and waited impatiently until she put food on the table.

The pet flap flapped, and when she looked up, she saw that a small procession of cats traipsed in. They had the decency to look extremely guilty, and so they should.

"Is there anything we can do?" asked Dooley.

"I think you did quite enough for one day, wouldn't you say, Dooley?" asked Gran, putting a touch of iron in her voice.

"Oh, don't be too harsh on him, Ma," said Mom. "He wasn't to know that inviting Stewart would bring all of his friends and family, did he?"

"Is that how it happened?" asked Odelia.

Dooley nodded sadly. "I only invited Stewart because he said he was an orphan and didn't have a place to stay. And then when we weren't looking, he must have invited all of his brothers and sisters and nieces and nephews and assorted family, because the place was suddenly full of birds."

"And they didn't let me eat a single one of them," Brutus lamented. "Even though there were plenty to go around for everyone."

"I told you, birds are our friends, Brutus," said Max sternly. "And we don't eat our friends, do we?"

"I guess not," said Brutus, though it was clear he wouldn't have minded making an exception for birds.

"Better wait outside," said Mom. "It will be a while before we're ready in here."

"I'm sorry, Odelia," said Dooley ruefully.

"That's all right, Dooley," she said. Dooley was such a sweetheart it was simply impossible to be mad with him. "We'll get the house clean again. Just you wait and see."

Marge got up from the floor and took off her gloves. "I better check next door to see what our guest is up to," she said, giving Gran a not-so-friendly look. She motioned at her daughter. "I won't be long, honey. Just have to put some fresh sheets on the bed in the spare bedroom and clean up a little. We've been using the room as storage space, since we so rarely have guests." And after giving her mother another unhappy look, she hurried out, before their guest found himself in a house that wasn't as hospitable as he would have liked.

"I don't know what got into Marge all of a sudden," said Gran. "I bring home a nice doctor for Tex to play with, and all she can do is give me these nasty looks and bite my head off. Jeff is a brain surgeon, you know."

"Your house guest is a brain surgeon?" she asked. She wondered if she could get him to do an interview. She had been thinking about writing something about the medical conference but had yet to find a great angle. A brain surgeon staying at the house was definitely something she could use.

"See? At least you appreciate it when I bring home a guest," said Gran. She patted her cheek, leaving a smudge of bird poop on her face. "Good thing you're nothing like your mother, honey."

Odelia didn't know whether this was a compliment or not but decided not to dwell on it.

"You know, we probably should collect all this," said Gran after a moment.

"Collect what?" asked Odelia.

"Well, this bird poop, of course. There was this documentary on the Discovery Channel the other night about bird poop being worth its weight in gold. It's used in farming, you know."

"That's guano," said Chase. "Bat poop. This is ordinary bird poop, Vesta. So I don't think it's worth its weight in gold like you say."

"I know what I saw, sonny boy, and this stuff is worth a pretty penny. So let's not chuck it out, all right? Collect it in buckets and sell it to Farmer Giles when we have the chance. Trust me, he'll pay a great price for it."

And as Odelia glanced over to the old lady, she saw her face had lit up with a smile. It was an expression she was very familiar with and spelled trouble with a capital T!

CHAPTER 12

Fifi was particularly proud of what her human had accomplished. She couldn't stop talking about it.

"That flute playing was amazing, wasn't it?" she gushed. "I think he's probably the most amazingly talented man that I've ever met in my life."

I would have told her that she hadn't met a lot of people in her life, but that wouldn't have been a nice thing to say. Besides, her pretty enthusiasm was so infectious that a wide smile spontaneously lit up my own face when I watched her speak about her human in such glowing terms.

"I think I did my bit as well," said Harriet. "Don't you think I did my bit, snuggle bug?"

"Absolutely," said Brutus. "We all did our bit, and together we managed to get rid of those foul birds." He sighed wistfully, and I could tell that he was still dreaming of the moment he managed to get one of those birds between his slavering jaws. But there would be no birds on the menu today—and probably not any day, since in this household we like birds. Not to eat, but to communicate with and to treat as friends.

Our humans were still inside, cleaning up the mess that the birds had made, and as we chatted with Fifi, another neighbor joined our small company in the form of Rufus.

"You won't believe what happened to me," he said. I had a hard time understanding what he was saying since there appeared to be an obstruction lodged between his teeth in the form of a piece of fabric.

"You have a speech impediment, Rufus," said Fifi. "It's that thing between your teeth."

"Oh, this," he said and carefully dropped it down on the ground in front of us and then lay down on top of it, guarding it with his life. "That's what I wanted to talk to you guys about. These two men showed up on our doorstep and they tried to convince Marcie that she had to pay a gnome tax. Have you ever heard of a gnome tax?"

"No, we haven't," I admitted. "Though the same two men also tried to make Gran pay the same gnome tax, and then tried the gag again on Marge, making her believe she had to pay a bird tax."

"Pretty soon now Odelia will have to pay a cat tax," said Brutus, shaking his head. "The things the government gets up to extract more money from the population."

"Oh, but these weren't actually government agents," I told our friend. "They were crooks."

"I chased them away," said Rufus proudly. "I chased them away but not before grabbing a trophy in the form of this piece of cloth here." He gestured with his head to the piece of cloth on the ground. "It was part of the guy's pants, and now it's mine."

We stared at the piece, and I didn't like to think what kind of animal it would take to willingly walk around with a piece of pants in its mouth.

"Rufus, you have to throw it away!" said Fifi. "Who knows where that has been!"

"I know exactly where it has been," said Rufus. "Around that crook's buttocks. It's my trophy, so I'm not getting rid of it." He frowned. "Don't you guys collect trophies?"

I thought for a moment, but then shook my head. "I don't think so. I mean, I don't know all the cats in the world, but I don't think cats are in the habit of collecting trophies."

"I definitely don't collect trophies," said Harriet. "Though I do collect good reviews. Did you hear my recital just now, Rufus? How many stars would you rate it?"

"I'm afraid I missed it," said Rufus. "I did hear a fire alarm going off a little while ago, but then it stopped."

I had a feeling that fire alarm might have been Harriet, but decided not to elucidate. Harriet doesn't like it when we cast aspersions on her talent as a songstress.

"Maybe you should bury it," said Fifi. "I always bury my trophies."

"I thought that was bones?" asked Brutus.

"Well, bones and trophies, of course," said Fifi.

"Where do you bury your bones?" asked Rufus. "I like to bury them in different places, as you never know if someone will find them, and so if they find one, at least I still have all the others."

"Oh, I like to bury them all in the same place," said Fifi. "Kurt is the kind of person who doesn't like it when anyone enters his private property, and so I don't have to worry about anyone finding my little haul."

It was a good argument, and I found it exhilarating to have a first-row seat while two dogs discussed the intricacies of their trade as bone buriers. It isn't the kind of thing cats get into, so this was definitely a look behind the curtain for us.

Gran now exited the house, and judging from the excited

look on her face, had just had another one of her brilliant ideas. "You guys!" she said as she joined us. "I just had the most amazing idea!" She looked around. "Where are the birds?"

"Gone," I said.

"And good riddance, too," said Brutus.

"No, but we need them back," said Gran. "Do you realize what this is?"

She took a bucket from behind her back and showed it to us. One sniff and I knew exactly what it was: bird poop.

I made a face. "Best to throw that out, Gran."

"Maybe dump it on Tex's compost heap," Dooley suggested. "They do say bird poop is good for the compost heap, don't they?"

But Gran's eyes were glittering, and I had the idea that she had a different destination in mind for the poop. "Do you remember that documentary we watched together, Dooley? The one about the guano?"

Dooley thought for a moment, but then brightened. "Oh, absolutely! The Mafia don who managed to escape from his Mexican prison by digging a tunnel, right?"

"No, that was Juano," said Gran. "Guano is bird poop. It's the new gold. People will pay large sums of money to get their hands on the stuff." She held up the bucket. "And we've got it here for the taking, you guys!"

"But... isn't guano bat poop?" I asked.

"Bats are birds," she said. "So it's the same thing."

"I don't think so," I said.

"Look, wise-ass," she said, taking a stance. "Who is the adult here? You or me?"

I got the feeling that it might be me, but from long association with Gran, I knew that it's no use trying to talk her out of an idea once it's firmly lodged in that recalcitrant cranium of hers, so I merely shrugged.

"We're collecting guano," she said determinedly. "And once we have a nice big pile of the stuff, we're selling it for big bucks." Unfortunately for her, she had swung that bucket a little too enthusiastically, causing the 'guano' to get dislodged and end up on top of her head.

But she didn't seem to mind. Instead, she laughed. "It's also good for your hair. Imagine the luxurious locks I'll have! Blond and glossy, just like in those shampoo commercials!"

"Better don't eat it," I advised. "Bird poop is full of bacteria and parasites. You might get sick."

But of course, Gran wasn't listening. "I love this stuff!" she cried, and actually licked a piece of it from her lips. She made a face. "Poo!" she said, and immediately spat it out again. "Yuck." Then she frowned. "You know? I think I've read somewhere that they turn bird poop into medicine. It probably cures all kinds of things, like gout and cancer." She gave Dooley an intent look. "You have to find Stewart, Dooley. You have to convince him to come back and bring his family along with him."

"But... I thought you wanted to get rid of Stewart," said Dooley, very much confused by this sudden about-face in his human.

"Get rid of him! Are you crazy? We *need* that bird! We *want* that bird! BRING ME THAT BIRD!"

"Yes, ma'am!" said Dooley, as he jumped to attention and saluted General Gran.

CHAPTER 13

Jeff inspected his new surroundings and found them wanting in some respects. The house itself was nice enough, and quite new, he thought, even though he wasn't a specialist, of course, but the room wasn't what he would have called suitable for a weekend's stay. For one thing, the bed was small, and the wardrobe was full of clothes. On the wall, several pictures had been suspended of a smallish cat with a beigeish-grayish hue. All the pictures depicted the same cat, which made him suspect that the room wasn't a guest room as much as the private room of one of his hosts. His suspicions were confirmed when Marge Poole entered and gave him a horrified look.

He had taken a seat on the bed by then, and was looking around with a sort of fascinated surmise, his single suitcase on the floor next to him.

"Oh, my God!" said Marge. "I'm so sorry!"

He gave her a smile. "I'm sorry?"

"No, *I'm* sorry!"

"I mean, why are you sorry?"

"This isn't the guest room. This is my mother's room."

"Oh, I'm so sorry!" he cried, jumping up from the bed as if stung.

"You weren't to know," she said with an apologetic smile.

"When your mother told me to take the first room on the right, I thought…"

"She never could distinguish between right and wrong—I mean right and left. No, the guest room is across the hall."

He grabbed his suitcase and followed her out. "I already figured as much. With all the pictures of the same cat decorating the walls, I mean."

"That's Dooley," she said, then winced, as if she'd said something wrong.

He frowned. "Dooley? But I thought Dooley was a friend of the family?"

Without responding, she threw the door to the guest room wide. "This is it!" she said brightly. They both surveyed the mess that was piled high on the bed. Plenty of cardboard boxes and other detritus, possibly collected over the years. "We don't often have house guests," she said apologetically, and got busy removing the boxes.

"That's all right," he said. "All I need is a place to lay my head. I'll spend most of my time at the Star Hotel anyway. That's where the conference is."

"I didn't know my mother had invited you," Marge explained as she brought out fresh sheets and pillowcases and put them on the bed. "She didn't tell me. But then my mother doesn't often tell me what she's up to."

It caused a thrill of alarm to galvanize him. "Oh, but if you don't like me staying here I'll find some other place to stay, Mrs. Poole."

"Marge, please," she said. "And absolutely not. My mother invited you, and I wouldn't have it any other way."

"I tried to get a room at the Star Hotel," he explained. "But they were fully booked. I wasn't going to attend the conference at first, you see, but at the last minute, the organizers asked if I could give a seminar, since the person who was booked to give it couldn't make it. And so here I am."

"And we're glad to have you," said Marge warmly. It endeared him to the woman immediately. And as he glanced out of the window, he saw that he had been given a room at the front of the house, with a window overlooking the street, which looked nice enough. Across the street, he could look straight into the living room of the people living there, and he could even see a man reclined in his armchair reading his paper.

Small-town life. You just had to love it.

"I have to say I look forward to making your husband's acquaintance," he told his hostess. "One of the topics of this year's conference is the lack of family doctors, you see, and since I understand that your husband is a family doctor, I'm extremely interested to hear his views on the matter."

"Tex has been practicing family medicine for twenty-five years," Marge said as she quickly and efficiently replaced the sheets on the bed and fluffed up the pillow. "You can put your belongings in that cabinet over there," she said. "There's plenty of space. At least," she added after she had pulled open the cabinet and glanced inside, "after I remove some of this junk." She took out a stack of binders and shoved them underneath the bed. "There," she said with satisfaction, "that should do the job."

"Thanks so much, Marge. I appreciate it."

She gave him a radiant smile. "How long will you be staying? Ma didn't mention it."

"Oh, it's just the weekend," he assured her. "Monday, I'll be gone again."

"You mentioned earlier that your car broke down?"

"It did. It was a rental, and I already called the rental

company to have it picked up. They said they'll deliver a new one to the house so I should be all set soon."

"And settled in," she said. "How are you fixed for dinner?"

"Oh, I haven't decided yet," he admitted. "I thought about checking out the downtown area tonight. Maybe you could recommend a restaurant?"

"Nonsense," she said. "You will eat with us, of course."

"I really don't want to impose," he said, holding up his hands.

"No imposition whatsoever. Do you have a favorite dish?"

And as they discussed possible dinner options, his initial qualms about staying with the Pooles dissolved like snow on a sunny day. Vesta Muffin might have a slight touch of eccentricity, but the same couldn't be said about her daughter, who was one of the loveliest people he had ever met.

"If you'd like to take a shower," she said, "I'll show you the bathroom." And as she led the way, she added, "Please make yourself at home, Jeff. You're part of the family now."

"Thanks, Marge," he said gratefully. "Thanks so much."

When he had called Matilda earlier, the moment his phone was recharged, she had expressed her concern about his decision to go and stay with complete strangers, but he could reassure her now that everything was fine.

* * *

As Marge left Jeff to freshen up a little, she wondered whether to return to the library. But then decided against it. She didn't feel comfortable leaving the doctor alone in the house. He had made a favorable impression on her, but it wasn't right to leave him all alone. And since she was home now anyway, she might as well make sure he settled in all right. But first she had to help Odelia return her house from the ruin that it was back to its former state.

And so she went in search of her mother, to keep an eye on Jeff. When she couldn't find her, she wondered what the old lady could be up to now. When she ran into Max, sunning himself on the deck, she had her answer.

"She's looking for the birds," he said.

"Looking for the birds? What do you mean?"

"She wants to ask them to poop for her some more," he said, not making any sense at all. "She believes bird poop is worth its weight in gold and wants to collect as much of it as she can, and sell it to the highest bidder."

"She said something about guano?" said Dooley.

Marge rolled her eyes. "Oh, God. As long as she doesn't let them come anywhere near the house again, she can do whatever she wants." Then she got an idea. "Could you keep an eye on Jeff for me for the time being? I don't feel comfortable with him staying at the house unsupervised. And I really need to help Odelia finish putting her house in order."

"Absolutely," said Max.

"Who is Jeff?" asked Dooley.

"He's the brain surgeon that Gran invited," Max explained.

"Oh, I thought he was a child," said Dooley. "Him being unsupervised and all?"

She smiled. "Just make sure he doesn't get up to anything," she said.

He claimed he was a brain surgeon, but after the incident with those two crooks pretending to be IRS agents, she figured it was better to be careful.

And as the cats hurried off to the house, she returned indoors to help Odelia and Chase clean up their home. Even Grace was pitching in by scooping bird poop off the floor and depositing it into a bucket. It was a plastic bucket, and her scoop was one of the scoops she used at the beach, but it was still cute to see her do her bit.

"Ma wants to collect bird poop," she told her daughter. "So let's not throw this stuff out just yet, shall we?"

"I know," said Chase with a grin. "She called it liquid gold. And when I told her that bird poop isn't the same as guano, she got very upset."

"It's true that bird poop is a great fertilizer, though," said Odelia. "And I'm sure Farmer Giles will be happy to take the stuff off our hands."

"But he won't pay through the nose for it," said Chase.

"Just a token sum. Or maybe we could ask for some tomatoes in return."

"He does have great tomatoes," Chase agreed. "For my bolognese sauce. With some fresh parmesan." He kissed the tips of his fingers. "To die for."

Moments later, Marge was back to scrubbing more of the yucky, sticky, smelly stuff off the floor. The notion that they might get money for the bird excrement did put her in a slightly mellower mood, she had to say.

CHAPTER 14

Stewart might be a bird, but he had his pride. And so when that cat Dooley came after him and begged him to come back, his first instinct was to tell him to take a hike. But then the little fellow looked at him with those begging eyes, and even though he wanted to say no, his heart wasn't made of stone, after all, and so he gave in.

"Oh, all right," he said. "But this time don't spring any surprises on me, you hear?"

"What surprises?" asked Dooley.

"That fire engine wailing away and scaring us all off!"

"Oh, but that wasn't a fire engine," Dooley assured him. "That was Harriet. She has a very loud voice."

"I'll say."

Next to Dooley, who had taken up position underneath the tree Stewart had picked as his sojourn for the rest of the day, and maybe even the night, Max sat, and since the big orange cat struck him as the brains of the outfit, he decided to run it by him as well. "Do you think this is a good idea?"

"Absolutely," said Max. "But you can't stay at the house, Stewart. It's too much of a fuss if you do. You see, our human is very particular about hygiene and cleanliness, and after you and your family pass through, the place looks more like a pigsty than a home fit for human habitation."

He should have been insulted by this, since everyone knows that pigs are filthy animals, but there was some kernel of truth to it, he had to admit. "Okay, so what do you suggest?"

"We happen to have a very nice and spacious garden house at our disposal, so we would like to put you in there. And then you can poop as much as you want."

"A garden house, huh? And what about the food situation?"

"Same as agreed," said Max, proving himself to be an excellent negotiator. "You'll get all the food you need for as long as you need it."

"Look, this is all well and good," said Stewart. "But I've taken a look at Tex Poole's garden house. I even peeked inside, and that ain't what I would call spacious, Max. That thing is cramped! I'm not sure I'll manage to convince my brothers and sisters to go in there."

"Oh, but I wasn't referring to *that* garden house. I was referring to the garden house next door. It belongs to one of our other humans."

He rolled his eyes. "How many humans do you have?"

"Plenty," said Max with a smile. "Now this garden house has to be seen to be believed. It's huge and will be much more to your liking, I dare say."

"Okay, fine," he said, relenting. If there was free food in the offing, and free lodging, who was he to kick up a fuss? Even though these cats hadn't kept up their end of the bargain last time, Max struck him as sincere. It was true that humans are obsessed with hygiene, to the extent they might not like it when he and his family came to stay in their homes. "But I'm warning you. Any more funny business and I'm out of there."

"There will be no more funny business," said Max. "And that's a promise."

Something told him this cat could be trusted, so he streaked down from the tree and they shook paws on it—or rather: Max extended his paw and Stewart put his foot on it.

He just hoped he hadn't made a bad judgment call again.

And so the work of gathering the clan and directing them all to this majestic garden house that Max had talked about so highly began. It didn't take long, for birds love to eat, just like any other species, and the promise of an unlimited supply of bird food was very appealing to them. And if a couple of non-family members joined the throng, that couldn't be helped. In the end, he ended up gathering a rather large contingent. Possibly even larger than the last one.

And as they all flew in the direction of their new home, he could only see one possible flaw in Max's plan: a garden house has windows and a door, and so they would be effectively locked up in there, something no bird likes. But Max, being the shrewd operator that he was, had foreseen this. The moment they arrived and streaked down on top of the roof of the structure which, he had to admit, was indeed big and sturdily built, Max showed them a small window that didn't have any glass in it. Next to the window the small elderly lady stood that he had seen earlier. She was holding a brick in her hand and wore a smile on her face, and he got the impression that she had made sure that window didn't have any glass in it anymore.

"Welcome, welcome," she said. "Welcome to Vesta's Guano Farm!"

It was a strange name for a garden house, he thought, but then who was he to argue with humans? As everyone knows, they are one crazy species, and will do the strangest things for the strangest reasons. And so he flew straight into the garden house, and had to admit that he liked what he saw.

Lined up against one wall was a sort of trough, filled to capacity with bird seed in all manner and variety. The rest of the space was filled with the kind of things he loved to see: work benches, instruments neatly hanging from pegs on the walls, and plenty of shelves. Oh, how he loved shelves, and so, he knew, did the rest of his family. Great to perch on and do their business on. He picked one of the workbenches and thought that he would feel very much at home there. The place even smelled nice. Like pine. He loved pine. He loved to smell it, loved to sit on it, and loved to poop on it.

In other words: this new arrangement suited him very well indeed.

* * *

"It's working, Max," said Gran. "It's working just like you said!"

"I think there's even more than last time," I said proudly. It hadn't been easy to find Stewart and then to convince him to give the scheme another shot, but in the end the clan leader had seen reason, and had been able to collect an even greater contingent of the winged creatures than before.

"Now all we have to do is bring the buckets and harvest the guano every night and we're all set to make this guano farm a ringing success!" she said.

It was only because I love to see my humans happy that I had agreed to this scheme. But then I didn't see any harm in it either. The birds would be happy, since they got to have all the food they liked and had a nice place to stay. Gran might make a nice supplement for her pension, and use some of that money to buy stuff for the neighborhood watch, always a worthy cause. And Ted wouldn't mind that his garden house was being put to good use, as he didn't have much use for it himself, not being much of a gardener.

"Don't you think Ted Trapper will mind that we have loaned out his garden house to Gran's guano farm?" asked Dooley.

"I'm sure Ted will be only too happy that he can do his little bit for a good cause," I said.

"I still don't think it's fair that I can't sing anymore around the birds," said Harriet.

It had been the main stipulation that Stewart had insisted upon, and he had made it clear that it was non-negotiable. No more singing. And I could understand where he was coming from. Harriet's voice is an acquired taste, and even though we are used to it by now, I could imagine that for a novice hearing her sing for the first time must be like having to listen to a jumbo jet taking off, or, as Stewart had indicated, a fire engine en route to a raging inferno.

"Are you sure I can't have just one, Max?" asked Brutus as he watched intently as one bird after another tumbled into the garden house via the window whose pane Gran had conveniently removed. "I mean, one won't be missed."

"One will be missed, Brutus," I said. "Birds are like cats: would you like it if some big giant animal suddenly scooped up one of our friends and ate them?"

He thought about this for a moment. "Which friend?" But when I gave him a penetrating look, he relented. "Okay, fine. I guess I wouldn't like it if a great big animal ate one of my friends. Happy now?"

"What great big animals would eat our friends, Max?" asked Dooley, a look of concern on his furry face.

"It's just a figure of speech, Dooley," I said. "There is no big animal who will eat our friends."

"Are you sure?"

"Absolutely."

"A bear might do the trick," said Brutus, who doesn't possess some of the finer feelings the rest of us have. I blame it on the place where he used to live before he moved to Hampton Cove. He was born and bred in New York, after all. "Or a wolf, maybe? Though it would have to be one of our smaller friends. A wolf or a bear wouldn't eat Max, since he's too big and would get stuck in their throats." He grinned when I cut him a nasty look. "Just kidding! He wouldn't devour you whole, of course. First, he would rip you to little pieces before gobbling you up. So your size wouldn't be an impediment."

Dooley swallowed a lump at this word picture our friend had painted and didn't seem entirely at ease that no wolf or bear was eyeing us at that moment, ready to pounce.

"Okay, I think this is going to be the harvest to end all harvests," said Gran with satisfaction. But then she seemed to spot a fly in the ointment, for her face clouded. "Duck! It's Ted and he's heading this way!"

And to show us how it was done, she immediately ducked behind a tall rhododendron bush that Marcie Trapper had recently planted. The four of us scrambled for cover in a nearby shrub and awaited further developments. Fortunately, it proved to be a false alarm. For Ted wasn't about to enter his garden house but simply to spy on his neighbors, which is one of his favorite hobbies. We could see him glance across the hedge into Marge and Tex's backyard, and could hear Gran curse under her breath.

It's one of those things that are prevalent in the suburbs: neighbors spying on neighbors. Even in this time of binge-watching and the ubiquitousness of the smartphone, some things never go out of style.

Ted's wife Marcie now also joined him at the hedge. "Do you see him?" we could hear Marcie ask her husband.

"No, I think he must have gone inside," Ted said.

"Do you think it's a relative of Tex?"

"He did look like Tex," Ted said.

"Ooh, there he is!"

"Where?"

"I just saw him pass by the kitchen window. There he is again!"

"I see him."

They both stared intently, then Ted said, "I don't think he's related to Tex at all."

"No, he's too handsome for that."

"Marge, then?"

"Not a chance. Have you seen Vesta? If you want to know what a woman will look like twenty years from now, just look at her mother. This guy is a hunk, honey. And Vesta may be a lot of things, but beautiful she is not."

"No, I guess not," said Ted with a chuckle.

"Wait," she suddenly said, pricking up her ears. "Did you hear that?"

"Hear what?"

"Shush. It sounded like water boiling—behind us."

They both turned around to look in our direction. I could have told them that it was Gran and she did indeed produce a sound like water boiling, though in actual fact it was her head that was boiling, and she had a hard time suppressing the urgent desire to jump out from her hiding place and throttle both Ted and Marcie on the spot. It was a testament to her amazing and almost superhuman levels of self-control that she didn't.

The moment passed, and Ted and Marcie decided to return to the house. It was only when Rufus came sniffing at us and giving us a questioning look that I dared to breathe easy again.

"We've turned your garden house into a guano farm," I told the big sheepdog. "I hope you don't mind."

"A guano farm? What is a guano farm?"

"Birds, Rufus," I said.

"Gran wants to collect bird poop," Brutus explained when our canine friend still seemed oblivious. "And I can't eat them," he added sadly.

"Ooh, I like birds," said Rufus. "Can I play with them?"

Since I knew that for Rufus, playing with birds involved snapping at them, I didn't think this was advisable, and so I told him in no uncertain terms not to touch the birds. "In fact, don't go near them at all, Rufus."

"Oh, all right," he said. "But I can watch them, can't I?"

"Sure you can." And then I had one of those bright ideas I sometimes get. Brutus likes to say it's because my head is so big, so my brain must have adjusted itself to the size by filling it up to capacity. After all, nature abhors a vacuum. And so I said, "It's important to the success of our enterprise that Ted doesn't find out about this. So if you see him heading towards the garden house, you need to head him off, is that understood?"

"But how will I do that?"

"I don't know. Be creative."

"Maybe jump up against him," Harriet suggested. "Dogs are always jumping up against their humans, aren't they?"

"Yeah, I guess so," he said dubiously. But then he had it. "I'll simply ask him to play with the ball. I love to play with the ball, but Ted doesn't."

"He doesn't like to play with the ball?" I asked.

"No, he finds it tedious. Having to throw the ball and throw the ball and throw the ball? Says it's boring."

"The fool," said Brutus with a grin. "Who doesn't like to throw the ball and throw the ball and throw the ball?"

"Exactly what I said!" Rufus cried. "But does he listen? Of course not."

"Okay, great idea," I said, not wanting to get into an argument about the advantages and disadvantages of throwing a ball. To be honest, I wouldn't want to throw a ball about a hundred thousand times—or try to catch it, for that matter. But then I guess that's dogs for you: they never get tired of this particular pastime. "When you see Ted heading for the shed, get him to throw the ball. He'll get bored after a couple of times and head back inside."

"Okay, Max," said Rufus. "If you say so."

He didn't look happy, and I realized I had been too hard on him. "I'll ask Tex to play throw the ball around with you if you like. Or better yet, Chase. He loves dogs and he won't get bored. How does that sound?"

He smiled a blissful smile. "That sounds like heaven, Max."

And after I had made everybody happy this way, a warm feeling spread inside my chest. How much fun it is to spread a little sweetness and light!

CHAPTER 15

"Two hundred cakes! But the man is crazy!"

Clearly, Holly wasn't fully on board with the plan of Francis Reilly to bake two hundred red velvet cakes for the upcoming church raffle.

"You think it can't be done?" asked Hannah nervously. She and her two sisters were in the kitchen discussing the plans, with Norbert taking a nap upstairs.

"I guess it can be done," said Lee. "Though I'm not sure it *should* be done. I mean, I'm all for helping out Francis and doing what we can for the parish and that church roof, but this is practically akin to forced labor."

"Slave labor, more like it," said Holly. "Doesn't he have a baker who can take care of this? Does it have to be you?"

"I think Francis has asked all the favors he can ask of anyone," said Hannah. "At this point he's desperate to get the money to fix that roof."

"If Norbert hadn't messed up in the first place," said Holly as her lips formed a thin line, "this wouldn't be necessary."

"Harsh," said Lee. "But true," she admitted. "But then we

all know that Norbert has been a waste of space from the moment he was born."

"I'll bet even his mom and dad didn't like him," said Holly.

"Oh, they liked him, all right," said Hannah, who remembered her mother-in-law well, though not at all fondly, as the woman had been prejudiced against her from the start and never had a kind word to offer.

"Look, we better start planning," said Holly. "If we're going to do this, that is?" She looked at her two sisters for their opinions, and when both of them nodded, she sighed. "Okay, so I guess we are doing this." She rolled up her sleeves and grabbed pen and paper. "When does he need them, these two hundred cakes?"

And so the planning of the feast began, with Lee and Holly agreeing to pitch in on the day, so they would be able to meet the deadline.

"We probably should divide the work between our three ovens," said Holly, who had always been the most practical of the threesome. "That way, we're sure to be done on time. Though even then, I'm not sure how we will be able to manage." She thought for a moment. "Can't you ask Marge Poole to pitch in? And maybe Odelia?"

"I could ask them," Hannah said. "Though I'm not sure if they'll agree."

Over the years, some acrimony had crept into the relationship with her neighbors, mainly due to Norbert's intractable attitude towards the world in general and his neighbors in particular. Whereas once Hannah had aspired to have a great relationship with all the people on the block, Norbert hadn't shared these aspirations, and had alienated most of them by making a mountain out of every molehill at every possible opportunity. He had argued over parking spaces, had turned snitch on people parking too close to the curb, had yelled at people walking their dogs and not cleaning up their pup's poo, and had even turned Ted Trapper into a lifelong nemesis by once throwing a bucket of ice-cold water on his lovable dog when Rufus had come sniffing at the front door. Trick-or-treaters had always found a closed door on Halloween, and every block party had been routinely ignored.

"Look, all you have to do is ask them," Holly suggested.

"And make sure Norbert doesn't find out," Lee added.

"Yeah, or he'll make sure to sabotage the main event."

"Like he always does."

Hannah sighed and scratched her arm. Inadvertently, she had rolled up her sleeves, and when both her sisters gasped in horror and shock, she knew she probably shouldn't have done that.

"Hannah, what the heck!" Holly cried as she grabbed her sister's arm and twisted it so she could take a closer look at the large purple bruise that had formed there.

"I… hit it against the doorframe," she said lamely. But when Holly gave her a scathing look, she realized she wasn't fooling anyone. "I accidentally changed the channel on the television the other day," she admitted. "And Norbert didn't like it, as he was watching The Voice, and you know how much he loves The Voice."

"That man," said Lee through gritted teeth as she directed an angry look at the kitchen ceiling, above which her brother-in-law was napping.

"This time he's gone too far," said Holly.

"Oh, but it only happened once," said Hannah. But then Holly held up her other arm, where a yellow bruise was clearly visible.

"Oh, that," she said with a shrug. "Norbert didn't like that I forgot to wash his favorite shirt, just when he was getting ready to go bowling." She swallowed when she saw the look of pure hatred in both her sisters' eyes. "He doesn't usually get like this," she said. "Well, not anymore, I mean. He's a lot more relaxed lately."

"He shouldn't do this, ever," said Holly.

"That man is a monster," said Lee resolutely. "You have to do something, Hannah."

"File for divorce," Holly added.

She had been afraid this would happen, which is why she had decided not to say anything. But of course, her sisters had to go and find out.

"I don't want to get a divorce," she said lamely as she slumped a little. "And I don't want to go to the police either. I mean, it's such a big hassle. And they might not even believe me. Norbert will tell them it was an accident, and that will be that."

"That won't be what happens," said Holly.

"If they don't believe you, they're fools," said Lee.

Just then, there was a lot of stumbling overhead, and she knew that their loud voices had woken up her husband. And as they shared a look of suspense, footsteps sounded on the stairs, and moments later the man of the house stormed into the kitchen. He hoisted up his suspenders that were designed to hold up his pants and stared daggers at Hannah and her sisters. "Are you still here? I can't sleep with all the damn racket you women are making."

"It's the middle of the day, Norbert," said Holly.

The other two women were quiet, though, as both Hannah and Lee were afraid the guy might lose his temper. In fact, Holly was the only one of the three sisters who ever dared to talk back to the guy. Which also made her Norbert's least favorite person in Hannah's family.

"You," he said, pointing a finger at Holly. "Out of my house. And you," he added, pointing the finger at Lee. "Get lost. And you," he said, pointing his finger at Hannah. He then crooked his finger. "Come here. I've got a bone to pick with you."

Obediently, Hannah got up and followed her husband into the living room. But when she saw him remove his belt, she knew what was coming and made to leave the room.

"Stay!" he barked, as if she was a dog and not a human being. And since his voice held such a threat of violence, she figured it wasn't worth it to risk his ire any further by leaving. He hadn't counted on her sisters, though, who also walked into the living room and made a stand next to their sister.

Norbert smiled a cruel smile when he took in the opposition. "So that's how it's going to be, is it?"

"That's how it's going to be," said Holly.

"You lay one finger on her," said Lee, "and I'll…"

"You'll do what?" he said, smacking the palm of his hand with the belt. It made a decidedly sinister sound, Hannah thought, and she couldn't imagine what damage he could do with that thing, especially if he used the buckle, as he had done in the past.

"Better leave," she said quietly.

"We're not leaving," said Holly.

Norbert smiled savagely. "Looks like I've got some whipping to do. Better brace yourselves, ladies. Here she comes!"

And as he raised the belt high, suddenly Holly let out a blood-curdling scream, grabbed a nearby vase, and threw it at Norbert's head.

The vase connected and broke into a hundred little pieces.

For a moment, he just stood there, shaking his head like a dog, but then he growled, and it looked as if the move had made him more vicious than before. And as he stormed at them, his foot caught on the carpet and he went tumbling into the nearest solid object, hitting it head-on.

It was the small cabinet that Hannah had received from her mom and dad on the occasion of her wedding. It was small but solid, with a marble top and strewn with the kind of little knickknacks that she loved so much.

The knickknacks went flying, and as Norbert went down, she found herself staring at the smear of blood on the edge of that massive marble top. Then at the floor, where her husband of fifty-two years lay motionless.

For a moment, the three women didn't speak, then Lee bent down next to the guy and pressed a finger against his neck. When she looked up, Hannah knew what she was going to say before she said it.

"I think he's dead."

CHAPTER 16

Jeff had to say that he was enjoying his time with the Pooles tremendously. Doctor Poole had arrived home and the two men had spent a very pleasant dinner talking shop, with Tex explaining the intricacies and challenges of building and maintaining a small-town private practice as a family doctor. It certainly was a far cry from being a big-town brain surgeon like Jeff, or working at a hospital, but nevertheless extremely enlightening. So much so that he had asked Tex—and the man had accepted—to hold a presentation at the conference, since he was the one person who would be able to bring them the real-world view of the realities on the ground, so to speak.

After dinner, which had been superb, he had profusely thanked Marge, who was the most charming hostess imaginable, and had decided to go for a little walk. The sun had set, and the world had turned dark. As he walked along, he met a man walking a very large dog, which he recognized as a sheepdog. For some reason, the man stared at him intently and seemed on the verge of asking him something, but then thought better of it. Possibly one of Tex and Marge's neighbors, though he couldn't be sure, of course.

He had done a tour around the block, and had gone as far as the dog park, then returned via a field that looked like a prime candidate to build some more of the same fine houses on. Marge had told him that it belonged to a local businessman who was now spending some time as a guest of the state for crimes committed. A lot of the locals used it to walk their dogs there now, since it was overgrown with weeds and shrubs.

He was passing through a street parallel to Harrington Street when he experienced an urgent need to pee. Since he had no idea how far from home he was, and his bladder made it clear that there was no time to waste, he entered a small grouping of trees to do his business, unseen by anyone.

And he was just busy relieving himself when he happened to glance past the trees and witnessed the most curious sight: three women were carrying the body of a large man and placing him on the ground. One of the women then took out her phone and made a call, presumably to the police. Clearly, that poor man had met with an accident. And if Jeff hadn't been answering nature's call, he would have immediately volunteered his services as a doctor. Though upon closer inspection, the man looked beyond help.

And as he watched on, it wasn't long before more people descended upon the scene: a man dressed like a priest and a second man of smallish aspect dressed in a butcher's white smock.

He knew he probably should have left, for he was doing something that in all his life he had never done: being a peeping Tom and snooping on other people. But then the most amazing sight met his eyes. The man dressed like a butcher took out a big butcher's knife and started cutting up the dead man!

* * *

It isn't often that the Pooles entertain guests, but when they do, it certainly is the best kind of guest, for somehow Gran had managed to convince an actual brain surgeon to come and stay with us. Now I don't know exactly what it is that a brain surgeon does, but I can only imagine it's up there with the more important professions in the world.

"He must have very steady hands, Max," said Dooley as we sat on Marge and Tex's porch swing and watched the moon rise in the sky.

"Yeah, to operate on a brain he must have nerves of steel," said Brutus.

"I think he's very handsome," said Harriet dreamily. "And I'm only saying that as a general observation," she hastened to add when her mate gave her an odd look.

"He is a very attractive young doctor," I agreed. "And probably talented too, or he wouldn't have been invited to speak at this medical conference."

"They should have asked Tex," said Harriet. "He's a great doctor."

"Oh, haven't you heard?" said Brutus. "Jeff has asked Tex to speak at his conference. To offer him the view of a small-town family doctor."

"Isn't that absolutely wonderful?" said Harriet. "I'll bet he'll have a lot of very important things to say on the subject."

She was right. After all, Tex has been a small-town doctor for a great many years now. And as we thusly discussed the newest arrival in our family, the guest of the Pooles, the very man came shuffling around the corner and abruptly took a seat on the porch next to us. He was staring ahead of him with what are usually termed unseeing eyes, and I got the impression that there was something very wrong with him.

"Look at his hands, Max," said Dooley. "They're trembling."

"Look at his face," said Harriet. "It's contorted in fear!"

"And look at his jaw!" said Brutus. "It's on his chest!"

They were right. The surgeon, who had looked so happy and joyful when he had set out on his evening walk, looked as if he had seen a ghost.

We would have asked him what was wrong, but of course he couldn't understand us. He might be a brain surgeon, and as such an extremely accomplished and intelligent person, but the language of cats was a mystery to him, as it is to most humans.

"I think he needs a doctor," said Harriet.

"But he *is* a doctor," Dooley pointed out.

"Even doctors need doctors from time to time," I pointed out.

"But... can't he be his own doctor?" asked Harriet.

"I guess it's not that easy," I said.

"No, I guess he can't operate on his own brain," said Brutus. "Though maybe if he used a mirror, he could manage? Or two mirrors, probably."

Gran and Scarlett had walked out of the house, and when they spotted the doctor sitting there like a deathly pale and trembling wreck of a man, streaked forward to lend him support. "What's wrong?" asked Gran immediately.

He looked up. "Mh?"

"Did something happen?"

The doctor slowly shook his head. "Just when you think you've seen it all," he murmured.

"Move over, you guys," said Gran, and made us shift off the porch so she could sit next to the doctor.

"Do you want me to get Tex?" Scarlett suggested.

"See?" said Brutus triumphantly. "Even doctors need other doctors when they're not feeling well."

"Just tell us what happened, Jeff," said Gran.

"I just saw... a man... cutting up... another man," he said brokenly.

We shared a look of surprise. "Looks like he was present at an operation," said Harriet.

"Maybe he's temping at our local hospital," Brutus suggested.

"I'll bet that's it," said Dooley. "I mean, how many brain surgeons are there? Not a lot, I would think. They must have decided to take advantage of his presence here in Hampton Cove to perform urgent brain surgery on one of their patients."

But when I studied the man, I got a feeling that wasn't what he was referring to. And his words confirmed me in my view. He looked up, a look of horror on his handsome face. "I think I've just witnessed... a murder!"

CHAPTER 17

"The weird thing," said Jeff, "is that I think there was a priest present."

Gran and Scarlett exchanged a look of surprise. The only priest we know is Father Reilly, but he would never be instrumental in aiding and abetting a murderer. At least I didn't think he would.

"Where was this?" asked Gran.

Jeff gestured with his head to the house. "Across the street. I was going for a walk and I happened to pass by the backyard of one of the houses there, and that's when I saw it." He shivered visibly. "It was the worst thing I've ever seen in my entire life." He gave Gran an intense look. "We better tell Chase. He is a police detective, isn't he?"

But Gran held up her hand. "Not so fast. I think we better look into this first."

I could see where she was coming from. After all, if Father Reilly was implicated in a murder, it might not be a good idea to involve Chase, who has a habit of arresting anyone he suspects of stepping on the wrong side of the law, even if that person turns out to be the parish priest and one of Gran and Scarlett's closest friends.

"I think this is a case for the neighborhood watch. What do you think, Scarlett?"

"I definitely think this is a case for the neighborhood watch," Scarlett confirmed.

And so Gran placed a hand on the doctor's shoulder. "Fear not, Jeff. The watch is here. Now if you could do the honors and show us where you saw this grisly scene play out?"

And so it was that a brain surgeon from Seattle happened to lead a small procession consisting of two pensioners and four cats along the deserted streets of our pleasant neighborhood in search of a murderer and a priest officiating said murder.

It wasn't long before we arrived in the backyard in question, the scene of the crime, so to speak. I've often been present at crime scenes, but mostly only after the deed is done. Post-murder, not pre-murder or mid-murder. This might be the first time I was going to be present while the murderer was still busy cleaning up after himself, and trying to get rid of the body, if Jeff's words were true, which I didn't doubt they were, judging from the way he came across all discombobulated and flustered. Even the best actor can't fake that expression of shock and horror, and Jeff was not an actor.

"Over there," he whispered as we followed him into the bushes. I stuck my nose in the air when a pungent smell filled my nostrils and sniffed.

"Someone has been peeing here," Brutus remarked, and I had to agree with that assessment.

"Definitely human urine," Harriet confirmed.

"Maybe this is one of those places, you guys," said Dooley.

"You know, those places where a lot of people hang out? I've seen it on the news."

"Oh, you mean like a meeting place for young couples?" asked Harriet.

"Lover's lane," said Brutus with a smile. "Oh, does that bring back memories, you guys." But when Harriet gave him a curious look, he quickly wiped the smile from his face.

"What's a lover's lane, Max?" asked Dooley.

"Well, it's a lane," I said, "where lovers meet," I concluded a little lamely.

He shook his head. "They didn't mention a lane in the program I saw. Just that there are certain places where a lot of people go to pee. Mostly they're located close to certain public places like theme parks and concert halls. The people who live there say that people pee in their backyards, and even in their mailboxes. It was an item on the news."

I got a feeling that this was not that kind of place, though it certainly was feasible that the reason the good doctor had witnessed what he had witnessed was because he had ventured off the beaten track when the tide was high and he'd found himself with an urgent need to relieve himself of certain excess fluids. Which, if I wasn't mistaken, was a crime in and of itself. Though not as grave as murder, obviously.

We had arrived at the spot in question, and now saw that the brain surgeon hadn't been lying: a man was indeed doing something to another man, who was lying motionless on the ground, while three women stood nearby and also... Father Reilly.

I would have advised caution under these particular circumstances, as one never knows what a murderer will do when faced with stiff opposition in the form of two members of the neighborhood watch, but Gran clearly wasn't the kind of person to nurse these considerations. Instead, she came crashing out of the shrubbery like some minor dinosaur and walked straight up to the killer. Putting her hands on her hips, she eyed him sternly, like a schoolmarm confronting a student caught smoking in the toilets. "Well?" she demanded. "What do you have to say for yourself, young man?"

The guy looked up at this sudden intruder, then glanced over to Father Reilly, who came hurrying over. "Vesta, I didn't expect to see you here!"

"And I didn't expect to see you, Francis," Gran returned, quite cleverly, I thought. "What's going on? Did you just murder this poor man?"

"No, of course I didn't murder this man!" said Father Reilly. "How could you even think such a thing!"

"I see you, I see the dead man, and I see plenty of blood," she explained. "That's how I'm thinking such a thing!"

"Well, I didn't kill him," said the priest. And when Gran's gaze cut to the man on the ground next to the victim wielding the butcher's knife with practiced ease, he hastened to add, "And Benny didn't kill him either."

"So it's Benny, is it?"

Benny nodded and held up his hand. "Benny Dowd at your service."

Gran eyed the appendage with a look of distaste. "I'm not shaking that."

"Oh, I'm sorry," said Benny Dowd, and wiped his bloodied hand on his white smock and held it up again. "So nice to meet you, Mrs…"

"Muffin," said Vesta, slightly mollified. "Vesta Muffin." Murderer or not, the man had manners. So she made to shake his hand, then thought better of it and turned schoolmarm again. "So who killed him? I mean, he's obviously dead, and he didn't die from cardiac arrest or pneumonia, or his head wouldn't have that funny shape and there wouldn't be all this blood."

Father Reilly glanced over to the three ladies standing in a sort of huddle nearby. I recognized them as Hannah Dunlop and her two sisters, Holly and Lee, and the dead man on the ground as Norbert Dunlop. Not a pleasant man, I have to admit, and his passing wouldn't be a great loss. For one thing, he didn't like cats and would always chase us away the moment we came anywhere near his front yard. And when dogs peed or pooped on the sidewalk, he would threaten to call the cops. He once even turned the hose on us when he felt that we roamed too close to his property.

"So Hannah killed her husband, is that it?" asked Gran, correctly interpreting the priest's glance.

He nodded but then held up his hands. "It was an accident. He had taken off his belt and was going to give her a beating but before he could, he tripped over the carpet and hit his head against a marble cabinet top. So Hannah called me, and since I didn't want her to get into any trouble with the law, I asked Benny over here to jump in and help us—"

"Get rid of the body," Gran completed the sentence. She raised her eyes heavenward and shook her head. "Francis, Francis. You do know that this could get you in some serious trouble, don't you?"

"But it was an accident," he assured us. "I know Hannah, and she would never kill her husband—even though by all rights she probably should have, and a long time ago, too."

"Francis!" Gran said.

"The man was the devil in disguise! Satan personified!"

Gran relented. "Yeah, I know. Norbert was not a good man. Quite the opposite. Even when Jack was still alive, he would complain about the guy. Said he was a beast. He would get drunk and belligerent and start picking a fight with anyone who was in the vicinity. One time he even got into a fight with Jack and gave him a black eye."

Scarlett had now also tripped up and surveyed the scene

with an expression of horror on her face. "But that's Norbert!" she exclaimed.

"Shh!" said Francis. "Keep your voice down, will you? Or do you want the whole neighborhood to know?"

"Did you kill him, Francis?" asked Scarlett, who must have missed the conversation.

The priest threw up his hands. "Why does everybody immediately jump to the conclusion that I killed Norbert? Do I look like a killer to you?"

"Well, you are here," Scarlett pointed out. "And the dead man is also here, and I can't for a moment believe that Hannah would have done this. Unless…"

"Yes, Hannah did do this," Gran confirmed, drawing a gasp of shock from her friend. "But it was an accident. He was going to give her a beating with his belt but instead he tripped and hit his head."

"Divine justice," Father Reilly murmured, and looked appropriately guilty after he had uttered these words, which spoke of a point of view that probably isn't in the good book or being taught at the seminary.

"So what are you going to do now?" asked Gran.

Just then, Jeff came wandering up, looking very coy and not at all at ease.

Father Reilly started violently. "And who is this!" he demanded.

"Oh, this is Jeff," said Gran. "He's staying with us."

"He's a brain surgeon," Scarlett said. "And a very clever one, too. Isn't that right, Jeff? Tell us that story about how you operated on the President's brain that one time."

"Maybe not now," said Jeff, who had gone pretty white around the nostrils, I saw. Which surprised me, since he must be used to seeing a great deal of blood in his professional life. "Is he… quite dead?" he asked.

NIC SAINT

Gran pushed the dead man with her shoe. "Yeah, I think he is," she confirmed.

"Vesta!" said Father Reilly. "Have some respect for the dead!"

"Why? Norbert never had any respect for me when he was alive, so why should I have respect for him now that he's dead?"

"Nevertheless," said the priest, and intertwined his fingers for a moment of prayer.

Hannah and her sisters now also joined the conversation. "I'm so sorry this happened," said Hannah. "Vesta, you have to believe me when I tell you it was an accident."

"The man was a monster," said Holly. "He was going to beat us with his belt, you know."

"All three of us!" said Lee. "If you can believe it." She held out her hand. "Look at that. I'm still shaking!"

She was right. Her hand was indeed trembling. Which I could certainly understand, as it's not every day that your brother-in-law threatens to beat you with his belt. Certainly, Tex had never done such a thing to Charlene. But then again, if anyone dared to raise their hands against Charlene Butterwick in anger, he'd probably lose a couple of digits, as she frowns upon that type of behavior—as rightly she should.

"Okay, so what happens now?" asked Hannah as she bit her lip. "You'll probably call Alec now, won't you?"

"Not necessarily," said Gran as she thought for a moment.

"Will you please make up your mind?" said the man who was still crouched next to the body, a nice big knife in his hand. "I don't want to be here all night."

"And who is this gentleman, may I ask?" said Scarlett.

"This is Benny," said Gran. She turned to Father Reilly. "Who is he?"

"Benny is a former convict," said Father Reilly, "who I met when he first came to confession a couple of weeks ago. He's been a steady visitor ever since, and also a regular member of the ex-offender support group I organize."

"What were you in prison for?" asked Gran.

"Oh, this and that," said the man, not looking to advertise his crimes.

"Benny killed a man," said Father Reilly, who didn't share these reservations. "Or rather three men. Which is why I thought he might be a good fit to get rid of the body since he's been in this situation before."

Gran still didn't seem to fully agree with the priest's approach, but I got the impression she was warming to the idea. "So what were you planning to do?"

"Well, cut him up, I guess," said the young ex-con. "And throw the pieces in the river. Or maybe bury them here in his backyard."

"He used to be a butcher before he became a murderer," said Father Reilly. "So he really is the perfect man for the job, Vesta."

"The most difficult part is the legs," said the guy as he pointed to the dead man's sturdy pins. "To cut through that femur, you need the right equipment." He pointed to a leather satchel that contained several knives and hacksaws. "Good thing I never got rid of them. I figured they might come in handy once I was released, so I asked my mom to keep them for me." He grinned. "Got a lot of fond memories of those instruments."

"Okay, so maybe you should go right ahead," said Gran, quite surprisingly, I thought. "And chop the guy into little pieces. But I'm not fully convinced that burying him or throwing him in the river is a good idea. There is always the possibility of discovery. Once people notice that your husband has gone missing, Hannah, they will start asking questions. And before long, the cops will come looking, and then you better not have him spread all across your lawn, if you catch my drift. And the river? I don't think so."

"Amateur fishermen will hook an arm or a leg," Scarlett explained. "Or kids will find his head floating when they're playing in the water. Give them a nasty surprise."

Hannah winced. "So what do you suggest?"

"The best thing would be for Norbert to disappear forever," said Gran. "And the only way to accomplish that is by dissolving him in sulfuric acid. Isn't that correct, Jeff?"

The brain surgeon had been following the conversation keenly and seemed to have trouble processing what he was hearing. But when thusly addressed, he snapped out of his stupor. "Mh? Oh, yes, absolutely. Sulfuric acid should do the trick. Uh-huh. One hundred percent."

"I love sulfuric acid," said Benny with a nod. "I used it on those three fellas I whacked. Dissolved them in my bathtub until there was nothing left. Good times."

"The problem is where are we going to find enough of the stuff to get rid of a hefty fellow like Norbert?" asked Gran thoughtfully. But then she had it, evidenced by snapping her fingers. "Let's ask Wilbur!"

"Wilbur?" asked Benny.

"Wilbur Vickery. He runs the General Store. He'll know where to source the stuff."

"Oh," said Benny as he wiped his knife on his sleeve. I got the impression he was disappointed that he wouldn't get to practice the art and science of his chosen profession as a butcher, but Gran immediately put his mind at ease.

"So why don't you cut that body up into little pieces, Benny, and I'll get on the horn with Wilbur and get him to bring us a drum of sulfuric acid ASAP? That way we can get this over with tonight." She beamed at Hannah and her sisters. "The neighborhood watch always comes through, ladies!"

"It certainly does," said Hannah, who looked a little dazed, I thought. Then again, mostly the idea of a neighborhood watch is to prevent crime, not get rid of its consequences.

It was at this moment that Jeff cleared his throat and raised a hesitant finger. "I'm sorry, but I'm afraid I can't go along with this."

Gran should have foreseen this. Doctors swear an oath to preserve life, after all, not to mess around with dead bodies and sulfuric acid.

Gran narrowed her eyes at the surgeon. "What are you saying, Jeff?"

"I'm saying I can't accept your solution," he said, and even tilted his chin to show us that he wasn't kidding and was prepared to defend his position.

"Is that a fact?" said Gran, and I noticed how a note of coldness had crept into her voice. I give you a bed for the night, a hot meal and a place to stay, her tone seemed to indicate, and this is how you repay me?

"The man was a monster, Jeff," said Scarlett. "We all knew what he was like."

"He won't be missed," said Father Reilly. "And what's the use of destroying another life?" He pointed to Hannah, who now looked like a deer caught in the headlights.

Jeff considered these arguments but finally shook his head. "I'm sorry, but we have to report this to the police. A judge will hear Hannah's side of the story and will decide in her favor, I'm sure." He gestured to Benny, who was licking his knife for some reason and had closed his eyes in ecstasy. "Can't you see this isn't right? It just isn't."

Gran finally nodded. "I agree," she said, much to Jeff's elation.

"You agree?" he asked.

"Of course! We shouldn't be rash about this. We should sit down and talk it through."

Jeff stiffened. "I don't want to talk it through." He had taken out his phone.

"What are you doing?" asked Gran, narrowing her eyes at the man.

"I'm calling the police if you won't." And he started dialing 911.

This didn't go over well with the watch leader. And so she lowered her voice and said in a sort of undertone, "Grab him, Scarlett—grab him and don't let go!"

Scarlett, who hadn't been expecting this, was late in her reaction. It gave Jeff plenty of time to make a run for it, and he didn't waste time doing so.

Which is how a strange scene played out on Harrington Street that night: a brain surgeon was running for his life, chased by two pensioners, a priest, a homicidal maniac brandishing a very large knife, and four cats. The only ones not giving chase were the dead man's wife and her sisters since Gran had told them to guard the body.

CHAPTER 18

I don't know if you've ever been faced with a problem of conscience, but it's not a fun experience. On the one hand, I wanted to help Gran and catch this runaway surgeon, but on the other hand, I felt he probably had a point: maybe we should let the police handle this instead of bothering with drums of sulfuric acid and weird homicidal maniacs whose wet dream was to cut people up in creative ways. I mean, we were the neighborhood watch, after all, not the neighborhood death squad last time I looked.

And since we were wrestling with mixed emotions regarding this particular situation, we decided that instead of carrying out Gran's request, we would sit this one out.

"I don't think this is a good development, Max," said Dooley, and that was quite the understatement. "I mean, what if Gran catches Jeff and she decides to dissolve him in sulfuric acid also? Doesn't that make her a murderer? And if that is so, it will make us accessories to murder, won't it? And punishable by law?"

"Absolutely correct, Dooley," I said.

NIC SAINT

"Gran won't dissolve Jeff in sulfuric acid," said Brutus. "She won't go that far. Will she?"

Harriet shrugged. "Whatever the case, it's out of our paws now."

The four of us were seated on the little wall that divides our front yard from the street, and had been since we had seen Gran and her procession round the corner at the end of the street. I just hoped that when she returned, she wouldn't have Jeff in shackles, dragging him down the street like some ill-advised posse. It wouldn't go down well with the neighbors. Or Chase, since he frowns upon that sort of thing.

"Maybe we should talk to Odelia," said Harriet.

"Yeah, maybe we should," I agreed.

Gran had obviously gone off the reservation, carrying her loyalty to Father Reilly a little too far. Then again, what about our loyalty to Gran?

"This is a typical case of divided loyalties," said Brutus. "On the one hand, Gran is our human, and so we should do what she says. But on the other hand, Chase is also our human, and I can't imagine he would agree with this business of cutting people up and dissolving them in acid."

"No, I don't think any of that is in Chase's penal code," I said.

"What is Chase's penis code, Max?" asked Dooley.

Brutus sniggered, and I cut him a reproachful look. "The *penal* code are the laws concerning crimes and offenses and their punishment, Dooley."

"Oh, I see. I thought you were referring to Chase's penis and its code."

"Not... exactly."

At that moment, Marge came out of the house, and so did Tex. The latter was holding on to his glass of wine, which he likes to enjoy during dinner.

"Have you seen my mother?" asked Marge. "She left to have some fresh air and hasn't been back since."

We exchanged a glance, but then I decided that maybe it was time to speak up. "Gran is chasing Jeff," I said, therefore.

Marge stared at me. "She is chasing Jeff? Why?"

It was an obvious question, but not so easy to answer. "Well, he didn't agree with her assessment to get rid of Norbert Dunlop's body," I said.

"Norbert's body? Why, what happened to him?"

"His wife killed him," I said. "Though it would appear that it was accidental."

"Norbert is dead?"

"That's correct," said Harriet. "His body is lying across the street. In the backyard of their house."

"But... what does Jeff have to do with this?" asked Marge, also taking a seat next to us on that low wall. Tex stood nearby, sipping from his wine and looking dumbfounded, an expression he has mastered over the years.

We all turned to Dooley. "You explain," I suggested. Dooley has a way of explaining complicated topics in an easy-to-understand way.

Our friend took a deep breath as he collected his thoughts. "Well... there was a dead body, and a vicious killer who wanted to chop it up into little pieces, but he needed special equipment to do it, and then he was going to throw those little pieces into the river, but Scarlett didn't think this was a good idea as kids could find his head and they wouldn't like it, so Gran said Wilbur would find them some sulfuric acid and they could put it in a drum with the dead man and then he would disappear and the police would never find out he was dead and his wife would be off the hook." He took another deep breath and gave us a triumphant look. "Gee, I said the whole thing in one breath!"

"And in one sentence," I said with a smile.

"Well done, Dooley," said Brutus, giving him a pat on the back. "I couldn't have said it better."

"But but but…" Marge sputtered, and we now became aware of the fact that she didn't seem to understand what Dooley had just said. It was true that he probably should have used shorter sentences. Nobody likes a run-on sentence, especially a librarian like Marge, who is very particular about punctuation and has never met a period or a comma she doesn't like. "But but but," she continued to sputter.

"What's going on?" asked Tex. "What did they say?"

She slowly turned to her husband. "Norbert from across the road is dead. And Gran wants to dissolve him in sulfuric acid."

"Good thinking," he said, nodding. "Sulfuric acid will do the job." Then he frowned. "But wait a minute. Why does she want to dissolve him in acid? Wouldn't a nice old-fashioned burial be the better solution? Or a cremation, maybe?"

"And why is she chasing Jeff, of all people!" Marge cried.

"Dooley?" said Harriet. "Can you explain about Jeff, please?"

Dooley took another deep breath. "Okay, so Jeff doesn't want Gran to use sulfuric acid because he doesn't like the idea, because Jeff is a doctor, and doctors don't like getting rid of bodies but like to save them for posterity by putting them in little jars filled with formaldehyde so they can put them on their shelves and look at them and study them and show them to other doctors, and so he told Gran no and Gran told Scarlett they had to catch him so they can dissolve him in sulfuric acid also."

I got the impression he had embellished a little here and there, but it still gave us the gist of the situation. The CliffsNotes, in other words, which should have satisfied Marge. But Marge didn't seem satisfied, for she gulped some more.

And when she spoke again her voice sounded a little funny. "Ma wants to kill Jeff and put his body in sulfuric acid also!"

"Now why would she go and do a thing like that?" asked Tex with a frown. "I mean, the guy is a great brain surgeon, he told me so himself. And a good surgeon like that should be cherished not... Wait, did you say she wants to kill him?"

Marge nodded. "Because he doesn't want her to get rid of Norbert's body."

Just then, Odelia and Chase came walking out of the house. "What's going on?" asked Odelia. "Where did you all go off to all of a sudden?"

Marge gave her daughter a pained look. "Your grandmother has finally gone off her rocker," she said, placing a comforting hand on Odelia's arm. "We all knew that one day this moment would come, and it's happened."

"What do you mean? What did she do?"

"She's only gone and try to destroy the body of our neighbor! And when Jeff said he didn't agree, she tried to kill him!"

"What?!!!" both Odelia and Chase cried.

I would have corrected them and told them that this view was a little one-sided, but I got a feeling my opinions didn't matter anymore, as they had already formed their own. It often happens that way. Once an idea is firmly lodged in a person's head it's very hard to convince them otherwise.

Just then, Jeff came around the corner. He was going well and going fast, though I could tell that the effort was taxing him, judging by the beads of sweat on his brow and his labored breathing. But his pursuers were far behind, so he didn't have to worry about being caught anytime soon.

"Jeff!" Marge cried. "Over here!"

But the moment Jeff caught sight of us, he seemed to utter a sort of shriek or scream and redoubled his efforts. Soon he was nothing more than a dot on the horizon, and by the time Gran, Scarlett and Father Reilly had caught up, he was gone. They were in a lot worse shape than their quarry, and as they drew up in front of the house, practically collapsed on the lawn.

From across the road, Benny Dowd came ambling up.

"So where is the guy?" he asked now.

I saw that he'd ditched the knife and the white smock, which was probably a good idea, as the combo screamed serial killer.

"Who are you?" asked Tex.

"Benny Dowd," said Chase between gritted teeth. "So you're out, are you?"

"That's correct, detective," said Benny cheerfully. "Back on the straight and narrow, as you can see."

Chase produced a sort of growl that spoke of his lack of conviction in Benny's dedication to walk the straight and narrow, and he was probably right.

"I think we lost him," said Gran, panting heavily. "He was too fast for us."

"I wouldn't worry about him," said Scarlett. "I've got a hunch he won't talk."

It was only now that Gran noticed that her daughter was looking at her askance. "What's gotten into you?" she asked therefore.

"What's gotten into me!" Marge practically screamed. "What's gotten into you! What's all this about dissolving bodies in sulfuric acid!"

Chase's head whipped up as if stung. "What!" he grunted.

"Nothing to concern yourself with, Chase," said Gran.

"What bodies? What sulfuric acid?" Chase demanded.

"Just the one body," said Gran with a shrug, as if it wasn't such a big deal. "And it won't be missed, I can assure you."

"What body!" Chase yelled.

Gran rolled her eyes. "That's what you get when your granddaughter marries a cop."

PURRFECT GRAN

"It's Norbert Dunlop," Marge told Odelia. "Your grandmother tried to dissolve him in sulfuric acid!"

"Gran!" Odelia cried. "Are you nuts!"

"Not yet, but she's getting there fast," Tex murmured as he took another sip from his glass of wine. Of all the people present, he seemed the least affected by all of this hullabaloo. But then he had lived under the same roof with Gran for a great many years, so he was probably used to this by now.

"Look, it was an accident, all right?" said Gran. "She didn't kill him, but I know what you cops will think. That she murdered her husband and was trying to get away with it. When that couldn't be further from the truth."

"Where is the body?" asked Chase, trying to get his emotions under control with some effort.

"Across the street," said Scarlett, pointing to the home where Norbert and Hannah Dunlop had lived since just about forever.

"So are my services no longer needed?" asked Benny. "Cause if that's the case, please tell me so I can pack up and go home." He looked at Father Reilly for an answer, but the priest didn't seem to know either, for he merely held up his hands. "Bummer," said Benny as he stalked off across the street. Then he turned. "If you want me to get rid of another stiff for you, you have my number, Francis. Always a pleasure!"

Chase turned a pair of icy eyes on the priest, who prevaricated by uttering a few choice phrases like, "Wonderful young man, Benny Dowd. Fully reformed, I can assure you." And, "He'll take up his old profession again, or so he's told me. Got a well-paying job as a junior butcher now."

"God," said Chase as he rubbed his brow. "This family," he added, and then set foot across the road, in search of that mysterious body.

"So... we won't be needing that sulfuric acid?" asked Scarlett.

"No, I don't think we will," said Gran. "I have a feeling that Chase will take care of Norbert from now on. Not as discrete as acid, mind you, but just as reliable."

"One question remains," said Harriet. "Who will take care of Jeff?"

We glanced up at Gran, and judging from the set look of her mouth, I had a feeling that she'd happily volunteer for that particular assignment.

CHAPTER 19

"What was all the fuss about, do you think?" asked Marcie Tapper as she watched from her front room window the scene playing out on the street outside. "There was a lot of yelling and shouting, and now Chase has crossed the street and entered the Dunlop place."

"No idea," said Ted. Even though he often supported his wife's obsession with their neighbors, he wasn't feeling in the mood to spy on them right now. He was worried about Rufus, who had been behaving strangely lately. And since he probably loved that dog more than life itself—and had even been accused by his wife of caring more for the mutt than he did for her or their two daughters—he hoped that he wasn't sick or in any kind of distress. Even though Rufus was by no means an old dog, he wasn't a puppy anymore either, and so it was probably understandable that he would suffer some of the drawbacks associated with life as an adult dog.

He turned away from the window, where indeed a strange scene had been playing out, and decided to check in on Rufus. He found the sheepdog in the backyard, where he seemed to be guarding the garden house for some reason.

Oddly enough, every time Ted would approach the structure, Rufus put his front paws on his chest and barked up a storm. Then he would go and get his ball and drop it at his master's feet, eager for Ted to play with him.

He didn't mind playing catch with the lovable mutt, but what he wanted more than anything was to get rid of some of the mites that had been attaching themselves to his precious rose bushes. And if Rufus wasn't going to let him anywhere near his garden house, that was never going to happen. The only reason he could think that the dog was so eager to play fetch was that he wasn't feeling well, and so he had already called Vena and set up an appointment to take a look at the sheepdog.

He now picked up the ball and threw it across the hedge and into the Poole backyard. That should give Rufus pause, he thought.

The dog shot away like a bullet from a gun and crashed through the little gate he and Tex had agreed to install so they had access to each other's backyards, in case one or the other went on vacation and needed his neighbor to keep an eye on things.

And while Rufus was thusly engaged in trying to retrieve his ball, Ted quickly set foot for his garden house. He was going to zap those darn mites to kingdom come if it was the last thing he did. They should never have touched his rose bushes! The moment he opened the garden house, though, he was surprised at the bizarre smell that hung there. And when he flicked on the light, he saw to his surprise that his precious garden house was filled with birds. On the workbenches, on the shelves, on the floor... They were everywhere! Some of them even clung to the walls somehow and others were on the rafters. His jaw dropped as he took in the eerie scene, for all of those birds were staring at him with their beady eyes, their little heads turning to take him in.

"What the heckleberry..." he muttered. How had they... And then he saw it: one of the windows he had installed was broken. He now opened the door wide, determined to evict this horde from his personal property. But if he thought they would allow him to do so, he had another thing coming. Instead, they all rose as one bird and started attacking him, pecking at his hair, his hands, his clothes—wherever they could get him!

"Get off me!" he yelled as he tried to protect his face. "Get away from me, creeps!"

He ran from the scene and as he did, suddenly the assault stopped, and when he turned to look, the door of the garden house slammed shut and the bolt settled on the inside. He blinked, as he couldn't believe his own eyes. Had those birds just chased him from his own garden house and locked the door? But how was that even possible?

He felt a nudge against his leg, and when he looked down, he saw that Rufus sat on his haunches, having dropped his ball at his master's feet, and sat looking up at him with expectant eyes.

"Woof!" said the dog.

Ted wasn't in the mood to throw the ball, but since he was still so shaken by his recent experience, he automatically picked up the ball and threw it. Rufus produced a happy woofle and immediately shot off after it.

From the house, Marcie came hurrying out. "Ted!" she yelled before she had even reached him. "You'll never believe what happened!"

"You'll never believe what happened to me," he muttered as he couldn't take his eyes off his garden house. He had a feeling those birds were all watching him closely. Watching. Waiting. Biding their time until they got another chance to attack!

"What did you say?" she asked after she had joined him.

"Nothing," he said. She wouldn't believe him anyway. No one would.

"It's Norbert! He's dead. An ambulance just arrived and they carried him out of the house. Hannah was there, and she told me. Turns out he fell and hit his head. Dead!"

"Dead," he returned without much zeal.

"Just like that!"

"Just like that," he repeated mechanically.

"I mean, you just never know, do you, when your time has come. One moment he's watching *The Young and the Beautiful*, and the next he's gone. Poor Hannah. They were such a devoted couple, weren't they?"

"They were? Oh yes, they were. Absolutely."

"Ted, are you all right? You're acting real strange."

"I'm fine," he assured her. He then turned to the house. "Tell me all about Norbert, honey. How did he die, exactly?"

And as Marcie tapped into her inner chatterbox, he glanced over his shoulder at his garden house, and marveled at the menace that lurked within. The dark and winged evil.

CHAPTER 20

A new dawn broke, and I was glad for it. The sun came hesitantly but with a certain insistence that is her prerogative, peeping through the curtains. I stretched and yawned luxuriously, enjoying this quiet time before all hell broke loose again. Our humans were still fast asleep, and my friend Dooley was resting peacefully by my side at the foot of Odelia and Chase's bed. All in all, I thought I'd close my eyes again and enjoy some more of that pleasant slumber. But I hadn't counted on Harriet and Brutus rudely thwarting those plans by entering the room and hopping up onto the bed.

"Max, Jeff hasn't returned home from last night!" said Harriet.

"Yeah, his bed hasn't been slept in," said Brutus. "And now Marge is panicking, figuring that something must have happened to him. She even thinks..." He speared open his eyes to emphasize the importance of his next words. "She even thinks that Gran may have done something to him!"

"Marge actually thinks that she's harboring a killer under her roof," said Harriet. "Can you imagine? Gran, a killer?"

"I can imagine," I said before I realized what I was saying.

"Max!" Harriet cried. "How can you say that?"

"Are you actually accusing Gran of murdering Jeff?" asked Brutus.

"I don't know," I said, shaking my head. "I mean, we know that she wasn't happy when Jeff disagreed with her plans to get rid of Norbert's body. And when he took off like that, I got the impression that she wanted to make sure he wouldn't talk. So did she go after him and shut him up?"

"I don't believe it," said Harriet decidedly. "I don't believe for one second that Gran has it in her to murder a person."

"And also, she's the leader of the neighborhood watch," Brutus pointed out, as if somehow that made Gran immune to harboring homicidal feelings.

Dooley had also woken up from our jabbering and had been listening quietly. "Do you think Gran is a killer, Max?" he asked.

"I don't know, Dooley," I said. "But if Jeff has gone missing, that doesn't bode well for Gran, since she was the last person to see him alive, and she had voiced certain threats against the man."

For a moment, we digested this information, and since the best thing is always to get the message from the horse's mouth, so to speak, we decided to go in search of this particular horse and ask her what was going on.

And so we hopped from the bed, leaving Odelia and Chase to enjoy some more of their slumber until the alarm clock went off, and headed over to the next house to look in on Dooley's human.

"I can't believe Gran would do such a thing," said my friend now. "I mean, we all know that she's a little eccentric, but to murder a man? That takes a different mindset."

"It certainly does," I said. And frankly, I couldn't believe it either. But since we had arrived at Gran's room, we nudged

PURRFECT GRAN

open the door with our paws and entered. The old lady was asleep on the bed, but when the four of us hopped up onto her chest and sat there for a moment, it wasn't long before she returned to the land of wakefulness.

"Can you get off my chest?" she lamented. "Four cats is too much!"

And so we stepped off her chest. When Dooley stared at her intently, she grumbled, "All right. What is it? Out with it!"

"Gran, did you murder Jeff?" asked Dooley, seeing no need to beat about the bush.

"What? Are you kidding me right now? Of course I didn't kill Jeff!"

"But he's gone missing," said Harriet. "His bed hasn't been slept in and all of his stuff is still there, but of the man, no trace."

"You did say you wanted to get even with him," I pointed out.

"When did I say that? Do you have the evidence to back up these specious claims?" she demanded heatedly. "No? I thought as much. So I will thank you not to spread these filthy rumors about me."

"They aren't rumors if they're true," said Dooley.

Gran threw off the comforter in such a violent fashion that all four of us were thrown from the bed. "I don't have to listen to this nonsense," she said as she put her feet into her slippers and stomped off in the direction of the bathroom. And after she had closed the bathroom door with a slam, making sure that we couldn't grill her some more on the subject, it became clear to us that she wasn't prepared to discuss this like an adult.

"I think there's only one thing for us to do," said Harriet.

We all turned to her. "And what is that?" I asked.

"We have to find Jeff before Gran is accused of murdering him."

NIC SAINT

It seemed like a most reasonable solution to a vexing problem, and since we all knew that time was of the essence, we decided to get going immediately. Once outside, for a moment we weren't sure how to proceed. But once again, Harriet proved her perspicacity by suggesting that we ask our good friends Rufus and Fifi to do the honors.

"They are dogs," she pointed out, which proved how clever she really was.

So we first went in search of Fifi, and once we had found her—gnawing on a bone in front of her doghouse—we proceeded to the Trapper backyard, where we found Ted Trapper staring intently at his garden house, with a strange look on his face. Between Ted and the garden house lay Rufus, his paws on top of his ball, looking sad.

"He doesn't want to play with me anymore," Rufus lamented. "I tried to get him to play with me, but he simply refuses. Just like I told you he would, Max."

"We're looking for Jeff," Harriet explained. "And we would like you and Fifi to help us find him."

"Okay," said Rufus. But then he wavered. "Who's going to make sure Ted doesn't go near the garden house?"

"Oh, I wouldn't worry about that," said Brutus. "We will only be gone a short while."

"Until you have found Jeff," Harriet added.

"And besides, if it's true that Gran murdered Jeff, then she won't have time to harvest guano anymore," said Brutus. "Because she will be in prison."

Both Fifi and Rufus stared at the big black cat. "Gran murdered Jeff?" asked Fifi, her eyes widening to their maximum circumference.

"We're not sure yet," I said. "But there's a good chance that she did."

"With the assistance of Scarlett and Father Reilly," Dooley said.

"And then they made his body disappear in sulfuric acid," Brutus added.

"That they got from Wilbur," said Harriet.

"Oh, dear," said Rufus, and I felt that summed up things quite nicely.

CHAPTER 21

After Vesta had taken a nice long shower, she decided it was time to take a first look at her guano farm and see if she could already harvest some of that liquid gold. And so she set out of the house, glanced across the hedge, and was satisfied when she didn't see any sign of Ted or Marcie. The last thing she needed was for those two to mess up her plans to become a very rich woman—possibly the first guano millionaire in the world!

She had looked online for possible sources of use for that wonderful bird poop and had found many applications. It was obvious that farmers were pining for the stuff, willing to pay through the nose to get their hands on it. And since she would have lots and lots of guano, she just might become the number-one guano source in the state—maybe even the country!

Too bad that Tex's garden house was so tiny. Otherwise, she would have set it up as a second farm in a heartbeat. With so many birds to provide poop, she needed space to put them. More farms to feed the machine.

She opened the little door connecting both gardens and

snuck into the Trapper backyard, glanced left and right one more time, and tiptoed over to the garden house. The moment she had set foot inside, the birds all seemed extremely glad to see her.

"You recognize me, don't you?" she said as one of them fluttered down and perched on her shoulder. "Oh, aren't you cute? It's Stewart, isn't it?"

The bird seemed to nod and released a steady stream of tweets as she smiled and rubbed him across the tiny head. "You're such a sweetie. How are you doing in here? Not too hot or too cold? I've brought some great grub for you, by the way." And she proceeded to spread some of that bird feed into the large trough she had set up on one side of the garden house. As she glanced around, she saw that plenty of droppings were already in evidence, so she started scooping them up and depositing them in one of the metal buckets she had selected for that very purpose. She was so busy that she didn't even notice when the door silently opened and closed.

But then suddenly a cough sounded behind her, and she looked up and was startled to see that Ted Trapper was standing there!

"Ted," she said. "What are you doing here?"

"This is my garden house," he pointed out, and he probably had a case, since technically it was true that it was his garden house. He gestured at the birds distributed all across the small space. "These birds. They didn't attack you when you came in."

"Of course they didn't attack me," she said, cursing herself for not being more careful. She should have waited until nightfall before entering Ted's lair. Now she would have to explain to him about the guano—and maybe share some of those proceeds. Darn it! "Why would they attack me?"

"They attacked *me*," the accountant said plaintively. "I set one foot inside and they all started pecking at me. Pecking at my hair, pecking at my face, pecking at my—"

"Yes, yes, they were pecking at you. What's your point, Ted?"

"So why aren't they pecking at you?"

She shrugged. "How should I know? Maybe they recognize a friendly face when they see one?"

"But I'm a friendly face also," he said, still in that same whiny voice that irritated her so much. "Can't they sense that I mean them no harm?"

"I don't know, Ted. I guess they see you as a threat. What were you doing in here anyway?"

"It's my garden house!" he said, repeating a point he had made earlier. "I can come in here when I feel like it, can't I? That's the whole point of having a garden house, isn't it? That I can come and go whenever I want to?"

"Yes, yes, all right. No need to go all hysterical on me." She gave him a grudging look. "You're probably wondering what I'm doing in here?"

"The question has occurred to me."

"I like to feed the birds," she said.

"Feed the birds?"

"That's right. I like birds. Is that a crime?"

"But... can't you feed them someplace else? Why do you have to feed them in my garden house? Now I'll never be able to get rid of them!"

"Because it's nice and big and comfortable, all right? Because of you, Tex has that tiny, decrepit sad excuse of a garden house, remember?"

"It's not my fault that Tex is too cheap to buy himself a decent garden house," said Ted defensively. "And besides, he did buy himself a nice big garden house. You stayed there recently, didn't you, the lot of you?"

That was true enough. In response to Ted buying this

gigantic structure, Tex had bought himself what he thought was an even bigger one, only for it to be a Scandinavian mountain cabin, which he had then shipped to the Adirondacks. In other words, an inconvenient location for a guano farm since it was a pretty long commute.

"Can't we come to some kind of arrangement?" she now suggested. "You let me keep my birds here and you…" She thought fast. What could she possibly offer her neighbor that he would keep quiet to his wife about the guano business? She knew the moment Marcie became wise to the scheme she would start making trouble. She was that kind of person. "I'll make it worth your while," she said finally, and a little lamely, she had to admit.

"Worth my while how?" he asked. Then he started. "Oh, no, Vesta!" He waved his hands frantically. "I'm not interested in any of that!"

"Any of what?" she asked. "I haven't even said anything yet."

"I know what you were going to offer, and I don't want it," he said, squeezing his eyes shut. "You were going to offer me certain… favors, and I'm telling you I'm not interested."

She rolled her eyes. "Get your mind out of the gutter, Ted. I wasn't talking about that kind of favor."

"You weren't? Then what were you going to suggest?"

She smiled. "I'll offer you what you want most in life."

He seemed mildly intrigued. "You are? And what is that?"

"The chance to win the gnome war from Tex."

CHAPTER 22

"Are you sure this is the right direction?" asked Harriet.

We had been padding along the street for what felt like hours now, and still hadn't found a trace of the missing brain surgeon.

"Absolutely," said Fifi.

We had given both her and Rufus a few garments of clothing of the doctor to sniff, and immediately they had set off down the street, in the direction the doctor had gone last night. And even though at first I had good hopes that we would find him posthaste, I wasn't all that sure now.

"We've only been going for twenty minutes, Max," said Brutus. "Have a little faith in Fifi and Rufus, will you?"

"Has it only been twenty minutes?" I asked. I guess my sense of time must have slipped over the course of my last few investigations. Then again, since cats aren't allowed to wear watches I couldn't possibly be blamed for having a bad perception of time.

"I think we're heading in the direction of the downtown area," said Dooley.

"You're right, Dooley," said Harriet. "We're definitely going in that direction."

Traffic had picked up, and the sidewalks were teeming with people, so it stood to reason that we were nearing the heart of town, which is usually a lot busier than the streets around our house located in the suburbs.

Fifi and Rufus were still going strong, their noses to the ground and not giving up so easily. And lo and behold: we walked around a corner and found ourselves on Main Street all of a sudden!

"This is where he must have gone," said Harriet. "I can feel it in my bones."

"I thought he would have headed to the park," said Brutus. "To sleep on a bench, you know."

"Brain surgeons don't sleep on benches in parks, snuggle pooh," said Harriet. "They sleep in five-star hotels."

"They're rich, are they, these brain surgeons?" asked Brutus.

"Pretty much," I said. "People will pay through the nose to have their brains fixed. It's very important to have a brain that works well. Without it, you're sunk."

"I can imagine," said Brutus, scratching his scalp, under which his own brain lay, such as it was.

All of a sudden Fifi and Rufus stopped, right in front of the Star Hotel.

"Why did you stop?" asked Harriet, for she had bumped into Rufus. And since Brutus had bumped into her, I had bumped into Brutus and Dooley had bumped into me, we weren't all that happy with this break in the proceedings.

"I think this is where he must have gone," said Rufus.

I brightened. "You guys! That means Gran didn't murder him! He simply came to this hotel to see if they had a room for him."

"But I thought the hotel was fully booked?" asked Brutus.

"He's a brain surgeon, snow pea," said Harriet. "Brain surgeons always have a room whenever they want because you never know when your brain might malfunction and you'll need him. Every hotel manager knows this."

"You mean like a car mechanic, a plumber and an electrician?"

"Exactly! You need to keep these specialists on standby, honey muffin."

We looked up at the hotel facade, and I sincerely hoped we would find the brain specialist there, as it would exonerate our human. But then Fifi and Rufus moved around the back of the hotel, and entered an alleyway rife with dumpsters and all manner of garbage strewn about.

"Where are you going?" I asked.

"This is where the scent takes us," Fifi explained. "Isn't that right, Rufus?"

"It certainly is," the big sheepdog confirmed.

"Oh, no," I said. "But he shouldn't have come here. He should have gone inside and booked a room for the night!"

"Maybe the hotel was closed?" Brutus suggested.

"He must have slept in one of these dumpsters," said Harriet, inspecting the first dumpster we encountered. She stuck her head in. "Nothing," she said.

We went from dumpster to dumpster, but then all of a sudden I noticed that Fifi and Rufus had come to a standstill in front of a large metal drum. It had been painted blue and on it, a symbol had been painted of a skull and crossbones.

My heart sank. "Oh, no," I said.

"Oh, yes," said Fifi.

"Is this…"

"This is where the scent takes us," Fifi confirmed.

We all stood in front of the drum, as our worst suspicions were confirmed. I didn't want to say it but I knew I had to.

"You guys. Our human is a murderer!"

"This is horrible," said Brutus.

"This is terrible," said Harriet.

"What is in that drum?" asked Dooley.

I shared a look with Harriet, and she shook her head. Better not tell the little fellow, that look said. Better not tell him that Gran and Scarlett and Father Reilly must have grabbed Jeff off the street last night and deposited him inside this drum filled to the brim with sulfuric acid, to slowly dissolve until there was nothing left of him—not even his brain.

Just then, something moved inside one of the dumpsters, and a familiar face came peeping out.

"Hiya, fellas," said the face, and I smiled for I recognized Clarice, our good friend.

"Hey, Clarice," I said.

"What are you doing in the dumpster?" asked Harriet.

"Yeah, Scarlett not feeding you enough?" asked Brutus.

"Oh, you know how it is," she said as she jumped from the dumpster and deftly landed on the ground. "Sometimes you get homesick, so I like to come here from time to time, to my old stomping ground."

An idea occurred to me. "You wouldn't have seen Gran last night, would you?"

"And Scarlett?" Harriet added.

"And Father Reilly?" said Brutus.

Clarice frowned. "What time was this?"

"Oh, around… ten o'clock maybe?" I said. "Or elevenish?"

"Can't say that I did," she said. "Though by the time I got here it could have been later. Scarlett was out late last night, and when she didn't arrive home I figured I might as well hit the town. Why? Were they here?"

I shared a look with my friends, and decided that she probably should be told. "We think that Gran and Scarlett killed a man last night," I explained.

She gave an incredulous laugh. "Scarlett? Killed a man? Max, are you nuts?"

"No, but it's true," I gave the drum a tap with my paw. "These... are his mortal remains."

She stared at the drum. "But that's rainwater."

"I think you'll find that it's sulfuric acid," I said, pointing to the skull and crossbones.

"No, it's rainwater. I've seen it with my own eyes. It belongs to the hotel. The cleaners like to use it to wash the windows. It doesn't leave streaks."

I shook my head. "I'm afraid that your human is a murderer, Clarice," I said as gently as I knew how.

"She can't be. Scarlett is the sweetest, kindest soul on the planet. She couldn't possibly have suddenly turned into..." Then a thought occurred to her. "Who is she supposed to have killed?"

"A brain surgeon," said Dooley. "They didn't like it when he didn't allow them to dissolve another man in sulfuric acid, so they dissolved him in sulfuric acid."

"Impossible," said Clarice, but I could tell that she was starting to waver.

"I think we probably should get rid of the evidence," said Brutus. "Otherwise, Gran and Scarlett will be in trouble, and also Father Reilly."

I gave our friend a keen look. "Are you sure that we should protect them from discovery? I mean, they have killed a man."

"I know, but Gran is our human," he said. "We can't let her be caught. And what about Clarice?"

"What about me?" asked Clarice.

"What if Scarlett ends up having to serve time in prison? What's going to happen to you?"

"I wouldn't like to see Scarlett spend time in prison,"

Clarice agreed. "But if she does, I'll be fine. I can just move into these dumpsters again. I did it before, I can do it again."

"And what about Shanille?" asked Brutus. "She's not like Clarice. She can't go and live in a dumpster. She wouldn't survive."

"No, that's true," Clarice said. "Shanille wouldn't survive one night out here, surrounded by rats and all kinds of vermin."

It certainly was a tough call. Were we going to uphold the law and turn Gran and the others in? Or were we going to make sure the evidence of their crime disappeared? And what about Jeff? Didn't he have rights, too?

Like I said, a tough call! And as we stood there conferring, Kingman came waddling up to us. "I saw you guys schmoozing here," he said. "And I got curious to see what you were up to. So what are you up to?"

I figured we shouldn't keep any secrets from Kingman, especially since his own human was involved. "Gran and Scarlett and Father Reilly murdered a man last night," I explained therefore, "and asked Wilbur to provide them with a drum of sulfuric acid so they could dissolve his body." I tapped the drum. "That's him right here."

Kingman gulped. "In there?"

"In there," I confirmed. "Dead and dissolved."

"And Wilbur did this?"

"Wilbur did this," I said.

"My god!" he said. "I knew he was up to something when I arrived home last night after cat choir and he wasn't there. So that's what he was doing. Getting rid of dead bodies in the dead of night!"

"And here I thought that the neighborhood watch was supposed to keep us safe," said Fifi, who looked proud as a peacock for having retrieved the murder weapon in the form of the drum. "And instead, they're just another band of mobsters."

"Gran is not a mobster," said Dooley. "Is she, Max?"

"She shouldn't have done this, Dooley," I said. "She shouldn't have murdered that man just because he didn't agree with her."

"Gran always has been quick on the trigger," said Brutus.

Another member of our squad now came walking up. It was Shanille, and since she was Father Reilly's cat, we decided to fill her in on what was going on. After all, she was involved as well. If Father Reilly was caught for Jeff's murder, she would be without a home.

"I don't believe it," she said determinedly. "Father Reilly would never do this. Never!"

"Well, he did do it," I said. "And here is the evidence."

She glanced up at the drum. "Have you looked inside?"

"No, and I would advise you not to try," I said.

"It's filled with sulfuric acid," Rufus explained. "If you fall in, that's it. No more Shanille left. Just skin and bones."

"Not even skin and bones!" Fifi assured him. "Nothing!"

"Nothing? You mean everything is gone?"

"Absolutely everything. Sulfuric acid will make you disappear completely. Not even a single molecule left."

We all shivered at the thought of being dissolved like that. "I don't want to disappear, you guys," said Harriet. "What will the world do without my singing talent to liven things up? I wouldn't want to do that to the world."

"I'm still going to take a look," Shanille announced. And before we could stop her, she had jumped on top of a nearby dumpster, then onto a windowsill that had once served a window that was now bricked up. The sill was located directly over the drum, and as she balanced there, while the rest of us held our breaths and clutched our heads in terror, she peered into the drum.

For a moment, she seemed focused on the drum, and then she seemed to start. "My God!" she said.

"What is it?" asked Kingman. "Shanille, what is it!"

"There's something floating on top!"

"What?!" Kingman cried. "Shanille, don't keep us in suspense!"

"It… it looks like a piece of metal," she said.

Immediately, I flashed back to something Jeff had told us during dinner last night. That he'd had an accident as a kid and a part of his skull had been replaced with a metal plate. He'd even tapped against it and it did sound a little metallic, I had thought.

"It's Jeff!" I said. "It's the metal part of his skull!"

I closed my eyes, for my suspicions had been confirmed. Our very own human… was a vicious killer!

CHAPTER 23

Jeff Morrison, seated in the Star Hotel's dining room and about to start on his breakfast, happened to glance out of the window and wondered where he had seen those cats before. But then he had it: they were the cats belonging to the Pooles. He retracted his head with a grimace. Why did he ever think that they were the nicest, kindest people he had ever met? And then all of a sudden he was running for his life. It was almost like a scene from one of those horror movies where a couple arrives in a motel at night, and are in fear for their lives for the rest of the movie.

Good thing he'd had the common sense to head straight into town, and had the perspicacity to ask if they had a bed where he could lay his weary head, even if it was located in the broom cupboard. Lucky for him they had been able to put him up in one of their rooms, and he was glad for it.

He'd ask the manager to pick up his personal belongings from the Pooles later today, but at least he was safe from that crazy Vesta Muffin. He had already told the receptionist about his harrowing adventure, and the kid had told him

Mrs. Muffin had quite the reputation in town, and not a good one. But he had also told him that she was the chief of police's mother, and if he thought that he'd be able to file a complaint against her and be successful, he was a fool. And so he had decided to finish the conference and get out of Dodge! The last thing he needed was some vengeful cop making his life miserable or, worse, making him disappear!

He wondered how people could live in such a town. With murderers on the loose, protected by the local constabulary. It certainly wasn't the kind of thing he was used to. But since his breakfast was getting cold, he decided to put all thought of last night's harrowing events out of his mind and focus on his future, which was certainly a lot brighter than his past. He had been satisfied to discover that the hotel had gone all out and had provided a full breakfast for him, even though he had only checked in late last night. Now that was service for you, and evidence Vesta didn't control everything and everyone in Hampton Cove, like some kind of local mafia don.

And he would have taken his first sip of coffee when he suddenly spotted a familiar figure entering the dining room. It was none other than Scarlett Canyon, Vesta Muffin's number-one henchwoman!

Immediately, he ducked under the table and out of sight. Scarlett was accompanied by a young man who could have been her grandson, and they were heading his way! And as he extended his head for a moment, like a periscope on a submarine, he found to his horror and surprise that Scarlett had selected the next table for herself and her companion!

He quickly turned his back on her, and hoped she wouldn't recognize him. He knew he should have gotten the first cab out of town that morning! Such a fool he was, to believe he wouldn't bump into that gang of killers again! But since he couldn't very well get up now without drawing

NIC SAINT

attention to himself, he decided to finish his breakfast, and wait until the woman had left.

From time to time he glanced over his shoulder, and saw that she had ordered a full breakfast for herself and her boyfriend, who looked like a teenager, really. Such a disgrace. But what did he expect in a town like Hampton Cove!

One of his colleagues now entered the breakfast room and when he saw him, his face lit up and he came over. "Jeff Morrison!" he bellowed when he was thirty feet away.

Jeff made frantic motions for him to keep his voice down, but the damage was done. Suddenly Scarlett stood before him, and studied him closely.

"Hi, Jeff," she said. "I don't know if you remember me from last night?" She held out her hand. "Scarlett Canyon. I'm a friend of Vesta Muffin?"

"Mh?" he said, trying to look as casual as possible, while his eyes were scanning the room for anyone who could get him out of this predicament. Then he noticed that a knife was lying next to the butter, and he quickly snatched it up and held it in a death grip. Just in case she tried any funny business. "Oh, of course I remember you, Mrs. Canyon."

"This is my grandnephew Kevin," she said, and the kid waved at him without enthusiasm. "It's his birthday today, and so I promised to buy him a fancy breakfast here at the Star." She directed a look of concern at him. "How are you feeling today, Jeff? You had us all worried last night, you know, after you took off like that. You gave us quite the scare."

"Oh, fine, fine," he assured her. "Never better," he said, flashing a strained smile.

His colleague had joined them and now stood smiling at both Scarlett and Jeff, not knowing what to say. It was the lifeline Jeff had been looking for. "Bob!" he said, getting up, and gripped the man's hand and pumped it energetically. "Am I glad to see you!"

"Aren't you going to introduce us?" asked Bob, turning to Scarlett who, it had to be said, cut quite the attractive figure.

"Bob Lints, this is Scarlett Canyon," he said reluctantly. "Scarlett, Bob Lints—a colleague of mine. Bob is a cardiologist."

Scarlett smiled a wide smile. "So nice to meet you, Mr. Lints. I don't think I've ever met a cardiologist before. What is it that you do, exactly?"

"Well, I'm a cardiologist," he explained.

She blinked a few times, flashing a smile at the man. "Yes, but what do you *do*?"

The man looked deeply into Scarlett's peepers, and seemed entranced. "Hearts, my dear lady," he said. "I'm a specialist of the heart."

"Ooh, is that a fact? I'm also a specialist of the heart," she giggled. "I just love a great love story, don't you?" She turned to Jeff and placed a hand on his chest. "Oh, Jeffie, do you remember that promise you made? About that double date?"

"I did? Oh, I did! Of course I did." He gestured to Bob. "Well, Bob will only be too happy to have dinner with you, won't you, Bob?"

Anything to distract this monstrous woman and escape!

Bob's face lit up with an expression of sheer delight. "It would be my absolute honor to buy you dinner," he said. "But you mentioned a double date? For you and a friend?"

"Vesta Muffin," said Scarlett, and Jeff winced at the sound of that dreadful name.

"I could always ask Owen," the cardiologist suggested. "He's a podiatrist, you know. But don't let that give you the wrong idea. He's a great guy and a wonderful raconteur and will be a worthy dinner date for your friend."

"I'll tell her to meet you and Owen here… shall we say eight tonight?"

"It would be my absolute pleasure," said Bob, and actually went and pressed a kiss on the woman's hand!

Scarlett retook her seat next to her so-called grand-nephew—a likely story!—and in spite of the fact that Jeff was ravenous, he decided to skip breakfast and escape while he still could. And as he hurried out of the dining room, he almost bumped into Luca Adsett-Brown, the organizing committee chairman.

"Ah, Jeff!" said the man, and grasped him by the elbow. "I'm so much looking forward to your address I can't even begin to tell you—and so is every person I spoke to."

"About that, Luca," he began, but the man gripped his elbow even tighter and leaned in while he dropped his voice.

"Josh Burnside and Jackson Slocombe bailed on me, so I'm counting my lucky stars that I have you to fill in the gap. Could you possibly go a little longer? Or a lot?"

"Well…"

The chairman stared him right in the eye. "Help me out here, Jeff." It wasn't a request but an order, and Jeff understood that Luca was not the kind of man to disappoint. And so he nodded.

"Of course. Anything you want, Luca."

"Lifesaver," said the chairman, and gave him a clap on the shoulder for his trouble.

Looked as if he would have to stay in this town from hell a little longer. Hopefully, he would make it out of there alive!

CHAPTER 24

Marcie had to admit she wasn't all that happy with her husband. In all the years she had been married to Ted, she had always been aware of his faults and weaknesses, but never had she been more aware than now. For some reason that she didn't understand, he had been acting very strange lately. Withdrawn and jumpy. And when she asked him what was wrong, he claimed that everything was fine—just A-okay. Clearly, that was a bold-faced lie since everything was not A-okay.

And then there was the schmoozing with Vesta Muffin. She and Ted had never been big fans of the woman, but now it was almost as if she had become Ted's go-to person to talk about all things gnomes. Which was another thing that irked her: this whole obsession with his gnomes was frankly starting to get on her nerves. It had been fun for a while, with the girls even gifting their dad funny-looking gnomes for his birthday and as Christmas gifts. Leila had even given him a Christmas sweater with a big gnome on it and they had all laughed.

It wasn't so funny now. He had been coming and going to

the garden center and returned home with several new gnomes—massive ones, bigger than the ones he already had, and the backyard was literally littered with the hideous creatures. So much so that she wondered if her husband had finally lost his final marble and had gone crazy. Gnome-crazy.

She was even considering consulting with Marge Poole, whose husband was also a self-confessed gnome nut, about what to do about this affliction Ted was suffering from. As she stood gazing out of the kitchen window, watching her husband position another one of his gnomes just so, and making sure that it overlooked the little brook he had installed in the backyard, she shook her head in dismay.

Just then, the doorbell rang, and she sincerely hoped it wasn't the UPS man with another shipment of those monstrous creatures. She had a good mind to tell him to take them all back and destroy them. Dump them in a landfill for all she cared. Get rid of them once and for all. No woman should have to put up with this kind of nonsense.

She stalked down the corridor and into the hallway to open the door, and was greatly surprised to find the same two morons standing before her—the ones that had pretended to be IRS agents collecting a so-called gnome tax. This time they were wearing mustaches, but that didn't fool her for even a single second.

"What do you want?" she asked, not making any effort to be polite.

"Cooper and Jackson, ma'am," said the tallest of the two, holding up a badge. "IRS agents. It has come to our attention that you have a lot of birds in your backyard. Are you aware that the governor of this fine state has recently issued a bird tax?" He took out a document and tapped it smartly. "And according to our information, you haven't paid your bird tax yet."

"Oh, go away," she said, and made to slam the door on the duo. Unfortunately, the smallest of the two, a thickset individual with a ridiculous mustache, put his foot between the door and pushed it open.

"This is not to be taken lightly, ma'am," he said. "There are large fines connected with the non-payment of the taxes owed to the government."

"We will now proceed to count the number of birds in your backyard," the tall one said. "And based on that, we will issue you a statement with the appropriate tax and interest accrued."

"You will do no such thing," she said viciously. "And if you don't go away, I will call the police."

The small one closed his eyes and gave her an indulgent smile. "Threatening an IRS agent is a crime, Mrs. Trapper."

Just then, she saw Chase drive up, so she waved at him. The moment the two so-called IRS agents caught sight of the cop in his squad car, they immediately went as white as sheets and couldn't move away from her door fast enough. By the time Chase had joined her, they were long gone.

"Those two so-called IRS agents were here again," she told the cop, who looked a little harried, she thought. Which wasn't a surprise, as not only did he have to wrangle Hampton Cove's entire criminal population but also his own family, who probably gave him even more trouble than the collected crooks the town featured. "This time they wanted to count the number of birds in my backyard and give me a fine for not paying my bird tax."

"I arrested them," said Chase. "But unfortunately, the judge let them walk. Turns out they got a pretty good lawyer."

"So arrest them again. This is a clear violation of the conditions of their bail, isn't it?"

"It is," Chase confirmed. He glanced past her, and frowned. "Is that Ted I hear singing?"

She sighed deeply. "I need to talk to your mother-in-law about him. He's gone full gnome on me again. Been collecting the figurines like crazy. He's bought no less than twenty new ones in the past twenty-four hours and if this keeps up I won't be able to walk in our backyard anymore without stepping on one of those horrible things."

Chase grinned. "Tex suffered from the same affliction for a while, but he seems to have calmed down considerably. I don't think he's bought any new gnomes for a while now, and he got rid of most of them."

"Good for him," she said. "What's Marge's secret? How did she convince him to stop collecting those things?"

"I think the disease simply burned itself out. Especially after that business with Blake Carrington and the gnome wars."

She remembered all too well. Tex and Ted had really gone toe-to-toe that time. "I think Ted hasn't gotten the message the gnome war is over," she said.

"I'm sure it will all work out," said Chase, but she wasn't so sure about that.

He bid her adieu and told her that if she saw those IRS fellas again, she should call him immediately and he'd make the arrest.

Closing the door and returning to the kitchen, she was surprised to see that of her husband there was not a single trace. And as she stepped out of the house and into the backyard, she couldn't find him anywhere. It was only when she happened to glance across the fence that she saw her husband moving about in the Poole backyard, a big hammer in his hand, demolishing one of Tex Poole's largest gnomes.

CHAPTER 25

When Vesta got the call, she was out of the office in a heartbeat. Tex yelled after her, "Where are you going?" and she yelled back, "Take care of some unfinished business!"

It didn't take her long to get to the Star Hotel, where Scarlett met her in the lobby. She was accompanied by her grandnephew Kevin, the computer nerd.

"It's Kevin's birthday today," Scarlett explained. "And we always have breakfast here at the Star for his birthday."

"It's a family tradition," said Kevin.

Vesta noticed how the teenager's eyes were sparkling with merriment. "What's so funny?" she asked.

"Oh, nothing," said the kid. "Just that Auntie Scarlett explained to me how you two chased a man last night but he got away." He chuckled freely. "I wish I had been there. And I wish I could have filmed it on my phone and turned it into a TikTok video."

"Ha ha," said Vesta, who wasn't in a great mood. Not only had Ted discovered her secret guano farm, but this whole business with Norbert and the sulfuric acid thing didn't sit well with her. After Chase had discovered what they had been up to, he had given the members of the watch a stern talking-to. The worst part was that he was going to tell everything to Alec, and she just knew what he would have to say about it.

Which made it all the more important they got a chance to sit down with Jeff and talk things through. She had wanted to talk to the man last night, but because he was determined to make a nuisance of himself, had asked Scarlett to restrain him while they did. Unfortunately he'd been quicker off the mark, and had managed to escape.

And to think she had opened her own home to that man. Clearly, gratefulness was an alien concept to the guy.

"Where is he?" she asked, getting down to business as was her habit.

"I saw him in the dining room just now," said Scarlett. "But before I got the chance to talk to him, he skedaddled."

"Gone like the wind," said Kevin, still chuckling freely. "I'll bet he's halfway back to Seattle by now."

"No, he isn't, you wise-ass," said Vesta. "He's got a conference to attend and a speech to give, so he has to be around here somewhere." The odd thing was that he hadn't picked up his personal belongings yet, which were still at the house. Then again, brain surgeons probably made a lot of dough, so he probably had money to burn on a new suitcase and a fresh set of clothes.

"I already asked at reception," said Scarlett. "And they put him in one of the maid's rooms, since the rest of the hotel is booked solid." She gestured to the bank of elevators. "Shall we go and see him now? He's probably in his room."

"Yeah, let's," she said, and the trio set foot for the elevator. "We should have asked Francis to tag along," she said as she applied her finger to the elevator call button. "He told me last night that he felt bad for the way we left things with Jeff."

"He only had himself to blame," said Scarlett with a shrug. "Why he had to run off like that is still a mystery to me." She turned to her grandnephew. "Was it just my imagination, or did he act funny just now as well?"

"Oh, it wasn't your imagination, Auntie Scarlett," said the kid. "That guy definitely was acting real funny. Almost as if he was mortally afraid of you."

"Can't imagine why," Scarlett muttered. At which point Kevin let rip a guffaw so loud and hearty that it made both ladies frown in dismay and plenty of guests loitering in the lobby turn to stare in their direction.

The elevator took them up to the third floor, where a number of rooms were reserved for the staff in case they had to stay the night for whatever reason. As they stalked along the corridor, checking the numbers on the doors, Vesta thought this was a part of the hotel she had never been in before. It certainly was a lot dingier than she had expected, but then hotel management probably didn't want to spend money on accommodation for its staff when they could spend it on adding another suite on the top floor.

"Number three-sixteen—this is it," she said, and without awaiting her companions' response applied her knuckles to the door. "Jeff!" she bellowed for good measure. "I know you're in there! We need to talk!"

When there was no response, she put her ear to the door and listened intently. "He's definitely in there. I can hear him moving around. Jeff!" she said as she gave the door a vicious pounding. "Open this door right now!"

"I told you, he's probably halfway back to Seattle by now," said Kevin with a wide shit-eating grin.

"And why would he do that?" asked Scarlett.

"Oh, don't listen to him," said Vesta. "He's just joshing with us."

"I'm not joshing with you," Kevin assured them. "Just

think, Auntie Scarlett. First you want to dissolve a man in acid, then this guy says he can't go along with your crazy scheme, and the next thing he's doing a runner and you're all chasing him. The poor man is afraid for his life!"

"No way would he be afraid of us," said Vesta. "What a strange idea, Kevin."

A maid was passing through the corridor pushing a cleaning trolley, and Vesta beckoned her over. "Can you open this door please, miss? We think something may have happened to the man inside. A heart attack, probably."

"Oh, no," said the maid as she hurried to open the door for them. "And he's such a nice man, too. A brain surgeon, he told me."

"Please step aside," Vesta advised the moment the door swung open. Immediately she charged in, and caught a flapping piece of pants in the window. "Jeff, no!" she yelled. And as she streaked to the window to stop the man from taking his own life, she found herself grabbing the first thing she could lay her hands on. Which, to her surprise, was a toupee. She stared at it dumbly, but then Scarlett was there, trying to talk Jeff off the ledge.

"Don't do this, Jeff," she implored him. "You've still got your whole life ahead of you. You've got a family, for crying out loud!"

"Don't come any closer!" the brain surgeon implored as he stepped further along the ledge.

"Don't jump," Vesta now also added her voice to the choir. "Things are never darker than before the dawn, Jeff! The sun will come out again! I promise you!"

"Stop right there!" Jeff cried as Scarlett put one foot on the ledge. "I'm warning you!"

"Oh, Jeff," said Scarlett. "Why don't we all go inside and sit down so we can talk about this? I'm a good listener, I promise you, and so is Vesta. You can tell us all about your troubles and we won't judge."

"I never judge," said Vesta. "I'm a very non-judgmental type of person. For one thing, I don't judge you for running away from us last night. I still don't know why you did it, especially after I opened my home to you and welcomed you into my family, but hey—I'm sure you had your reasons."

Just then, Vesta noticed movement down below in the alleyway this room looked out on. And when she looked closer, she saw it was the cats. They all seemed surprised to see her, so she gave them a wave. "Hey, you guys!" she called out. And to Scarlett, "Look, honey. It's the cats."

"And two dogs," Scarlett said.

"Fifi and Rufus," said Vesta, nodding.

"Gran, why did you do it!" Dooley was yelling for some reason.

"Hey, honey!" she yelled back. "What did I do?"

"Why did you kill that poor man and dissolve his body in acid?"

"Hard to hear from up here," she told Scarlett. "Though it sounds as if they want to know why we dissolved Norbert in acid."

"Tell them we didn't," Scarlett advised. But then she saw that Jeff stood staring at them intently, and revised her earlier statement. "Or maybe better don't." She lowered her voice. "The walls have ears!" she said as she pointed to Jeff.

"I can hear you, you know!" said Jeff.

"I know," said Scarlett. "That's what I just said."

"You are crazy!" Jeff yelled. "Both of you! Crazy!"

Vesta wagged a finger at the guy. "Now now, Jeff. That's not very nice of you. Especially after I gave you a place to stay."

"And then tried to murder me!"

"What are you talking about? Nobody is trying to murder you."

"*You* are trying to murder me!"

"A minor misunderstanding," said Vesta with a shrug.

"All we want is to have a little chat," said Scarlett.

"So let's all go inside and we can talk this through," Vesta suggested.

For a moment, Jeff seemed to consider his options, but since he didn't have anywhere to go, as the ledge ended at the next windowsill and that window was closed shut, either he jumped, or he stayed out there indefinitely.

"Do you promise not to murder me?" he asked.

"Absolutely," said Vesta. "I haven't murdered anyone yet, and I'm too old to start now. How about you, Scarlett?"

"Oh, I'm not crazy about murdering people either," Scarlett assured the doctor. "Too messy for my taste."

"Though that sulfuric acid business sure sounds interesting," Vesta allowed. "Too bad Chase got wind of things and had to spoil everything."

The doctor didn't seem fully convinced, but decided to take a chance on them, and started shuffling back to safety. And he probably would have made it, if a pigeon hadn't swept down and attached itself to his face. And as he emitted a high shriek of surprise, and slapped at the pigeon, he lost his balance and toppled off the ledge, plummeting to the depths below.

CHAPTER 26

We saw the man fall to his death, and I have to say it surprised us even more than it horrified us. For wasn't this the very same Jeff Morrison? The brain surgeon who was supposed to be dead and dissolved in the drum of acid we were standing next to?

As he fell, we all keenly followed the trajectory of his fall, but it was only when Dooley yelled, "He's going to fall into the acid!" that we scrambled to get away.

Acid burns, and we did not want to get burned by that horrible liquid!

And so we all ran for cover. I was about ten feet away when the poor man plunged into the deadly concoction, and even though I got a few droplets on my person, I didn't think they burned. Then again, I have a thick coat of fur, and a little bit of acid wouldn't hurt me.

Harriet was in a worse shape, though, for she hadn't been quick enough off the mark and had received a moderate soaking.

"It's burning!" she screamed. "I'm burning!"

"Quick, put something on her!" Brutus cried as he hurried to her side.

But what could we put on her? The only solution was to douse her in water, and a large quantity of it, too.

"There's water in that dumpster!" Clarice yelled helpfully and quickly led Harriet to the dumpster. A hop and a skip, and the white Persian was inside, submerging herself in the mucky brackish substance that was contained in the receptacle. It had rained a couple of days ago, and whoever this dumpster belonged to had forgotten to close the lid, so an ample volume of rain had settled in there, to mix with the garbage and refuse that had already accrued.

"This is so yucky!" we could hear Harriet scream from inside the dumpster. "Thanks very much, Clarice!"

"Hey, I saved your life, princess!" Clarice yelled back.

"Poor Jeff," said Dooley as we gathered around the drum of acid once again. "Looks like he died twice."

"How can a man be dissolved in acid, and then come back to be dissolved in acid again?" said Rufus, voicing a thought that we all entertained at that dramatic moment.

But as we watched, suddenly the man erupted from the drum, sputtering and yelling and dispersing droplets of acid in all directions!

"Hey!" said Brutus. "Watch it, buddy!"

"He's alive!" said Dooley.

"He won't be for much longer," said Kingman, offering the pessimistic view.

But once more Jeff was determined to prove us wrong by climbing out of that drum. He was soaking wet but otherwise seemed unharmed. He certainly wasn't burning or anything.

"His skin," said Dooley. "It's not peeling, you guys."

Dooley was right. The man's epidermis was still firmly attached to his dermis, which was odd, considering that sulfuric acid is supposed to be extremely corrosive. The only thing that had gone missing was his hair, but then if I wasn't mistaken, it hadn't been there when he went into the drum. Possibly he had lost it overnight. Stress does that.

"Strange," said Shanille. "I mean, good for him, of course." She seemed disappointed, and I guess we were all feeling a little bit of a letdown. If a man falls into a drum of dangerous and highly lethal acid and then crawls out of it as if nothing happened, it's not something that should happen.

And so Shanille stepped up to the guy. "Hey, mister. Why aren't you dead?"

"Yeah, you're supposed to be dead," Kingman chimed in.

"Guys, guys," I said. "It's not Jeff's fault that he isn't dead." Which is when I had one of those sudden brainwaves that I sometimes get. "Maybe there's no acid in the drum." Also, metal doesn't float, so I should have known that it wasn't Jeff in that drum.

Kingman, who had received an ample dose of the stuff on his person, gave a spot of it a tentative lick. Then he frowned. "You guys! Max is right. This isn't acid. It's water!"

"I told you," said Clarice. "It's rainwater. To wash the windows."

"Rainwater!" cried Harriet from inside the dumpster. "Did I really jump into a dumpster filled with garbage because of plain old rainwater?!"

We all grinned. "Afraid so, toots," said Clarice.

"This is your fault!" Harriet yelled as she came crawling out of the dumpster. She looked terrible, with banana peels dangling from her head, and some kind of sludge covering her from top to bottom.

"Oh, you poor thing," said Shanille. "Look at you."

"I'm going in that drum," said Harriet determinedly. "I am not licking all of this stuff off my person and giving myself gastritis!" And before our very eyes, she did a running start, then climbed all the way up Jeff's back, and jumped off the top of the surgeon's shiny bald head straight into the drum of 'acid.'

"But cupcake!" Brutus cried. "You'll get wet!"

"Better wet than filthy!" Harriet yelled back once she had re-emerged. For a moment she simply thrashed about, trying to get all of that muck off her person, then, cool as a cucumber, climbed out of her 'bath' again, jumped on top of Jeff's head once more, and made her way down the man, effectively using him like a ladder.

"Poor Jeff," said Shanille as we all watched the man, who looked nearer to tears than smiles of joy that he hadn't been dissolved in a drum of acid.

"Yeah, poor Jeff," Kingman agreed.

The surgeon seemed to have reached his limit, though, for he suddenly erupted into a stream of vituperative the likes of which I have seldom experienced and which I won't repeat here. The cursing was aimed at Gran and Scarlett, who were watching the scene unfold from an upstairs window.

"I'm so sorry about this, Jeff!" Scarlett yelled back.

"Yeah, we do apologize, Jeff," Gran added.

But Jeff wasn't to be appeased. Instead, he stalked off, soaking wet, his shoes making funny squelchy noises as he did, in the direction of the mouth of the alleyway, presumably in search of a towel and a fresh set of clothes.

"I think I'm fine, you guys," said Harriet, inspecting her person. "I think I got it all off me and I'm fine."

"Gran!" Dooley yelled. "There's no acid in this drum!"

"I know!" Gran yelled back. "It's a rainwater collector. The maids use it to clean the windows."

"So... where did you put that other man?" asked Brutus.

"What other man?"

"Well, Norbert from last night."

"He's at the coroner's office," said Gran. "Every suspicious death needs to be investigated, so the coroner came by to pick him up."

We all shared a look of surprise. "But... we thought that you put him in a drum of sulfuric acid!" said Harriet.

Gran smiled. "Turns out that's illegal, honey. Who knew!" She gave us a wave. "We better go and see what's going on with Jeff. I got a feeling that man might be madder than a wet hen." She gestured to Harriet. "Or a wet cat!"

And as she and Scarlett disappeared from view, we decided to leave. Harriet to allow her fur to dry and the rest of us to chew on the lessons we had learned over the course of our latest adventure. One thing stood out in my mind: never jump to conclusions!

And as we exited the alley, we saw that Uncle Alec had arrived, along with Chase and Odelia. They didn't look happy, and I had a feeling that Gran and Scarlett were both in for a rough ride.

CHAPTER 27

"That poor man," said Scarlett. "He's all wet."

"We have to find him a towel," said Vesta. She sincerely hoped that Jeff wouldn't have changed his mind about that double date he was going to set up for her and Scarlett. A cardiologist for Scarlett and a podiatrist for her. She didn't know what a podiatrist did, exactly, but she hoped it had something to do with the knees. She had been experiencing some minor knee pain since last night's chase and she wouldn't mind showing them to this man.

They had taken the elevator down to the lobby and when they couldn't immediately locate Jeff, she thought that they may have missed him. "Let's go back up," she suggested. "He's probably in his room."

"Good idea," said Scarlett.

"Stop! Wait!" a voice sounded behind them as they stepped into the elevator, but Vesta didn't pay it any mind. She hated when people tried to worm their way into an elevator when the doors were already closing. So rude. And so when a hand and a foot appeared and tried to wrench the doors back open, she smartly kicked the foot and gave the hand a knock.

"That should teach them," she muttered as both the hand and the foot retreated and the doors closed.

"That was your son whose foot you kicked," said Kevin.

"No, it wasn't," said Vesta. "Don't you think I'd recognize my own son?"

"It was him, and Chase, and I got a feeling they wanted to talk to you."

"Nonsense," she said. "Now why would they want to talk to me?" She gave her friend a critical look. "You really have to teach this kid some manners, honey. He keeps contradicting his elders."

Kevin actually guffawed at this, causing Vesta to rake him with a particularly scathing glance, which didn't seem to have any effect on the cheeky teenager whatsoever. Kids these days. No respect at all.

They had arrived on the second floor again and made a beeline for Jeff's room, hoping to find the man. When they got there, the door was closed again, which was a habit Vesta found extremely vexing. And since this time there wasn't a convenient maid on standby to open the door, they were stymied—but not for long.

Kevin proved his usefulness by taking a card out of his pocket and holding it up against the door. The door clicked and they were in.

"How did you do that?" asked Scarlett.

"Swiped it from the maid earlier," Kevin said. "I figured it might come in handy."

"Good boy," said Vesta, and squeezed his cheek between thumb and index finger, a gesture Kevin must have thought was funny, for he giggled. Strange kid.

The important thing was that they were in, and as they

hurried into the man's bedroom, she found that he wasn't there.

"Jeff?" she asked. "Jeff, where are you?"

She sincerely hoped he hadn't gotten that suicidal streak of his back and had ventured out onto the ledge again. Just to make sure, she hurried over to the window, but when she couldn't see him, she breathed a sigh of relief. "No man dies on my watch," she told her friend. "Not even if they're as eager as Jeff to take their own life."

"I wonder why he did that," said Scarlett as she sat down on the bed.

"Who knows?" said Vesta, throwing up her hands. "Could be family trouble, problems at work—anything." She shook her head. "I blame myself, you know. If only I had paid closer attention I could have seen this coming. I'm normally an extremely perceptive person, but I've been so busy with my guano farm I must have ignored the signs the man was hurting."

"Now where could he be?" asked Scarlett.

"Let me wash my hands, and then we'll head down to the lobby again," Vesta suggested. "Maybe he changed rooms."

As she opened the bathroom door, she suddenly found herself face to face with the missing doctor. The odd thing was that he was stark-naked, and when he saw her, started screaming up a storm!

"Don't be alarmed," she told him as she tried her very best not to look down... there. "Just let it all out, Jeff."

"Get away from me!" Jeff yelled.

"It's all right, son," she assured the man. "You can tell me anything. Anything at all. Trouble with a patient, issues of the heart. Vesta listens but doesn't judge. I run the Dear Gabi column in the *Gazette*, you see, so I've got an answer for any little problem you might be facing."

In response, the guy went berserk. Instead of taking his

time to tell her what could possibly be troubling him that was so bad he'd rather jump out of a window than talk about it, he streaked out of the bathroom and before she could stop him, had slammed out of the room.

"He's gone," she told Scarlett.

"I know!" said Scarlett, who looked a little dazed after coming face to face with the naked doctor.

"He didn't have a stitch on him!" Kevin cried happily.

"I know, Kevin," said Vesta. "Clearly the man isn't in a right state of mind, so it's important we catch him before he tries to hurl himself out of a window again."

And so they hurried from the room in pursuit of the troubled doctor. It wasn't hard to find out where he had gone, for he had left a trail of stunned-looking hotel guests behind, who all looked as if they had seen a ghost.

"He went that-a-way," an elderly lady declared as she clutched her necklace, as if afraid Jeff might rip it off.

And so they went that-a-way. Now if only the cats had been there, she thought, they might have a better chance at catching the guy. But of course, of the cats there was no sign. And then suddenly there was!

"Gran!" said Dooley as he popped out from behind a corner. "Max and I need to have a word with you."

"Not now, Dooley," she said. "We need to find Jeff. He's in a really bad way and we need to save him from himself."

Max was also there, she saw, and so were Harriet and Brutus. Scarlett's cat Clarice wasn't part of the contingent, and neither were Wilbur's cat Kingman or Francis's Shanille. Which was probably a good thing, as hotel owners get weird about a posse of cats on the premises. They frown at it.

And since cats are a lot quicker off the mark than humans, it wasn't long before her cats were running full-out in pursuit of the unfortunate doctor.

"They'll catch him," she told Scarlett and Kevin. "Just you wait and see."

"The question is, does he want to be caught?" said Kevin, once again being the wise-ass.

CHAPTER 28

"We have to save that poor man from Gran and Scarlett," I said.

"I thought Gran said to save him from himself?" asked Dooley.

"I get a feeling that Gran has things backward," I told my friend.

"How can we save a man from Gran?" asked Harriet. "I mean, it can't be done, Max."

I guess she was probably right. After all, cats shouldn't interfere in the affairs of man. That can only lead to disaster. But since I felt for the poor guy, I still figured we should give it a try.

We found the surgeon hiding under a bed in one of the empty rooms at the end of the corridor. A maid was cleaning the room and so the door had been left open.

"The poor guy," said Harriet. "He's not wearing any clothes. Why isn't he wearing any clothes, Max?"

"I'm not sure," I said. Why do people do things? It's hard to know why. Just then, the maid moved closer with her vacuum cleaner and as she glanced underneath the bed and saw the naked man, she opened her mouth and started screaming her head off.

"I guess she's wondering the same thing," said Brutus.

Jeff now pressed his index finger to his lips, in a bid to make the maid shut up, but it was to no avail.

"Pervert!" the maid screamed, and instead of using the vacuum cleaner to clean under the bed, she used it to poke at the naked man until he relented and crawled out from under there. "I'll call the police!" she warned him. "I know my rights, mister! You're like that Weinstein!"

"I'm not like Weinstein!" he assured her, but the fact that he wasn't wearing a thread didn't help his case. "I'm hiding from a crazy person who wants to kill me!"

"*You're* the crazy person!" she yelled. "Now get away from me!"

And since the doctor didn't have any other option, once again, he was on the run.

"This is just like that movie we saw the other night, Max," said Dooley. "Remember? With Harrison Ford? The doctor who was running and running and running and being chased by that cop? They thought he had killed his wife."

"I don't think Jeff has killed his wife," I said. But it was true that there was a certain resemblance. Especially when Jeff streaked past the elevator just as the doors opened and Uncle Alec and Chase stepped out. When they saw the naked man they did a double-take, but Jeff didn't even notice, keen as he was to get away.

"We're chasing the doctor," Dooley explained helpfully to Uncle Alec and Chase. "To protect him from himself."

"Or from Gran," I added.

Not that they could understand us, of course.

And since we didn't have time to stand there and chat, we hurried off again, in pursuit of the streaking doctor. We traced him to the other side of the hotel, where once again he had found a place to hide. This time he was in what looked like a dressing room for the hotel staff, for I could see several items of clothing hanging from hooks on the wall, benches placed beneath them with more items of clothes and shoes, and also a set of lockers where people could hang their personal belongings if they were more valuable.

Behind that, a shower room had been constructed, and it was there that Jeff had taken refuge now. He had secured himself a smartphone he must have found lying around and was dialing the emergency services, for he was yelling, "Police? You have to help me! I'm being chased by two vicious killers! Two old ladies who are both crazy and homicidal!" But then his eyes dropped to the floor and he saw the four of us. "It's you," he said. "You're the cats belonging to Vesta Muffin!"

"Easy now, Jeff," I said. "We're not going to hurt you."

"If you're here, she can't be far behind," the doctor said as his eyes darted this way and that. And then he barked into the phone. "Star Hotel. Please be quick. These people are absolutely vicious!" And then he hung up and proceeded to stare at us, a look of terror in his eyes.

"I think he's afraid of us, Max," said Dooley.

"Yeah, I would say so," I agreed.

"But why? We're just a couple of nice pussy cats."

"He's afraid of Gran," I explained. "He thinks she's going to put him in a drum of sulfuric acid, and he doesn't want that."

"Poor man," said Harriet. "He should know that Gran's bark is worse than her bite. And we should know, as she has barked at us many times."

She was right. Gran may have a tongue made of acid, but that doesn't mean she will put a man in a drum of acid.

"We did think that she actually murdered Jeff, though, didn't we?" Brutus reminded us.

"I think we all knew that couldn't possibly be true," said Harriet. "Deep down? Right?"

The truth was that we actually did think that Gran had murdered Jeff because he had seen too much. And even though we knew that we had made a mistake, it was easy to see why Jeff would think the same thing.

Just then, we heard Gran's voice in the hallway, and also Scarlett's. The look of fear on the man's face intensified, which is when I decided that it was time to put our money where our mouth was and help the guy out.

And so I held up my paws in a peaceable gesture and then hurried out of the personnel area.

"And? Did you find him?" asked Gran.

"He's not in there," I said. "But we met a poodle who says she saw him take the service elevator. So he could be anywhere."

Gran exchanged a look with Scarlett as she rubbed her chin. "He's probably in the kitchen," said the old lady. "Looking for an oven to put his head in. Suicidal people have a penchant for ovens, especially if they run on gas. Let's go."

And so they left, Kevin in their wake, to go look for the oven that Jeff must be eager to stick his head in.

Once they were gone, I breathed a sigh of relief. And as I looked down the corridor, I saw Uncle Alec and Chase come running. Looks like they were also chasing something, and if I wasn't mistaken, I had a hunch they were chasing Gran.

I pointed to the personnel area, and both cops nodded and went inside. Moments later, they had encountered Jeff, and even though the surgeon gave Chase a look of suspicion —he was part of Gran's family, after all—Uncle Alec quickly put him at ease when he introduced himself as the chief of police and showed him the badge to prove it.

They found some clothes so the man could get dressed, and then sat him down and asked him to tell his story.

They certainly got their money's worth, and got an earful from the surgeon. The main culprit in the story, as far as he was concerned, was Vesta Muffin. "The most deadly and batshit crazy woman I have ever met in my life!"

Judging from the look that the chief exchanged with his second-in-command, they didn't think he was wrong.

CHAPTER 29

When Tex arrived home after a long day at the office, the first thing he did was enter the kitchen and check the fridge for a snack and a can of soda pop. And as he popped the can of soda and happened to glance out of the kitchen window, his jaw dropped when he saw that all of his beloved gnomes were gone.

"M-m-marge?" he stammered.

"Yes, honey?" said his wife.

"My gnomes… did you remove my gnomes?"

"Your gnomes? No, I didn't touch them."

"But… they're gone. They're all gone."

Marge joined him at the window, and when she saw that he wasn't lying, looked as stunned as he was feeling.

"Do you think there's another gnome thief on the loose?" asked Tex.

"There was a couple of scammers going door to door yesterday," said Marge. "Demanding I pay a gnome tax."

"A gnome tax? I didn't know there was such a thing."

"There isn't. Like I said, they were scammers. Chase arrested them."

"Good." Suddenly Ted's head popped out over the fence, and then popped back out of sight. "Well, I'll be damned," he muttered, and without uttering another word, he stomped out of the kitchen and into his backyard. "Ted!" he demanded. "I can see you, you know!"

Ted's head popped back into view. The accountant had plastered a wide smile on his face. "Oh, hey, Tex. How are you, buddy? Busy day at the office?"

"What did you do to my gnomes?"

"Gnomes? What gnomes?"

"My gnomes! They're gone! All of them!"

"And here I thought you were finished with gnomes," said Ted.

"I was, until I wasn't," said Tex.

It was true that there had been a time when he had given up on collecting gnomes, figuring they were more trouble than they were worth. But the habit was stronger than himself, and so he hadn't been able to resist to buy a new gnome, and then another one, and another one, and now he was back to having a nice collection, dotting the backyard and providing some color and life to an otherwise pretty boring patch of lawn and shrubs.

"I don't see any gnomes," said Ted, glancing around pointedly.

"They were there, and now they're gone, and I know that you took them, Ted. So be a man and admit it!"

"Didn't anyone ever tell you that pointing at people is impolite, Tex?" asked Ted, and Tex noticed now that he was indeed pointing at the man. "Look, I have no idea what happened to your gnomes," said Ted. "I swear to God, neighbor."

He studied the man's face, and thought that he looked sincere enough. Still, Ted was an accountant, and accountants belong to the kind of species that can lie without flinching. In that sense, they are part of the same breed that has spawned politicians, bankers, and used car salesmen.

But since he didn't have any evidence to back up his accusations, there was nothing he could do and Ted knew it.

"Fine," he said. "But if you have any decency left in you, you will return my gnomes to me. Just put them in front of the garden house and I won't file charges, is that understood?"

Ted smiled and spread his arms. "Tex, buddy. I didn't take them, so how can I be expected to bring them back?"

"Just do it," he said, and he was pointing again.

And as he turned away from the hedge, he hoped that his words had been clear enough. Though why Ted would have decided to reignite the infamous gnome wars, he didn't know. Lately, he and his neighbor had gotten along a lot better, and now this. Then again, it's hard to look into a man's heart, and he knew that Ted Trapper's heart was as dark as they came.

* * *

TED TOOK another peek across the hedge and saw that his neighbor had returned to the house. He breathed a sigh of relief and leaned with his back against the hedge that divided his patch of paradise from his neighbor's. And as he stood there, something soft and wet touched the palm of his hand. When he looked down, he saw that Rufus was nuzzling his hand. Between the dog's legs was his ball.

"Not with that ball again!" he cried, and gave the ball a kick that landed it in the bushes. He stomped off in the direction of his garden house, and as he opened the door he glanced around to make sure that Marcie wasn't around. He certainly hoped that Vesta would keep her end of the bargain, and was already starting to wonder if the deal he had made was worth the trouble it was causing him.

The birds were still there, and as the floor and all of the surfaces were littered with poop, he thought that at least he couldn't be faulted for not taking care of his end.

Just then, the door opened and closed, and Marcie stood before him. When she saw the mess the birds had made, she gasped in shock.

"What is going on here!" she cried as she brought both hands to her face.

"I can explain," he said.

"You mean you purposely let these birds in?"

"It's Vesta's guano farm. She's collecting the bird poop so she can sell it for a lot of money to a local farmer. And in exchange, she promised that she would take care of Tex's gnomes. Make sure he stops collecting them."

Marcie gave him a look of incredulity. "So that's why you were destroying Tex's gnomes with that hammer!"

"She said she'd handle the fallout," he said. Only problem was that so far he hadn't seen any evidence of that handling. On the contrary. Now that Tex had given him that ultimatum, he wasn't entirely sure what he should do.

"Look, this gnome business has got to stop, Ted," said Marcie. "Both you and Tex need to grow up and stop acting like a couple of kids. So now I'm going to give you an ultimatum. Get rid of those gnomes of yours or else."

He should have known that Marcie had overheard his conversation with Tex. Marcie always heard everything, saw everything, knew everything. In that sense, she was as close to omnipresent and omniscient as it came.

"You don't mean that," he said, and gave her his best look of despair, which he knew always worked wonders.

She relented. "At least stop buying so many of them, Ted. Don't you have enough already? How many do you have?"

Not enough, he thought. Never enough. "Um, something like a hundred, maybe?"

"Well then. That's quite enough for any person, wouldn't you say?"

No, he wouldn't. "Yes, I guess so," he said instead.

"So what are you going to do about Tex's ultimatum?"

"Nothing," he said. "Vesta said she will arrange everything, and if she doesn't, she can't keep her birds in here anymore. That's the deal, and I'm keeping her to it."

"What a mess," said Marcie as she left the garden house, and he had the impression that she wasn't referring to the pile of bird poop covering all of his gardening tools.

CHAPTER 30

When Vesta arrived home that night, she wasn't in a good mood. Not only had Jeff told her and Scarlett in no uncertain terms that they could forget about that double date with his doctor friends, but Alec and Chase had sat her and Scarlett down in the lobby of the hotel and said some very unfriendly things. Not only about Jeff but also about the death of Norbert. According to Alec, they had handled this whole thing very badly when they had suggested that they dissolve the man's body in sulfuric acid. Alec had also told them not to go anywhere near Jeff Morrison ever again, and if they did, "I'll personally throw both of you in the slammer, is that understood!"

"You try to help someone," she grumbled under her breath as she entered the house through the kitchen door and opened the fridge. "And this is what you get. A lot of nonsense for your trouble."

"Ma," suddenly a voice sounded behind her.

She jumped about a foot in the air, as she hadn't seen Marge.

"You practically gave me heart failure!" she cried as she held a hand to her heaving chest.

"Good," said Marge, proving herself to be a very unloving daughter.

"Oh, now don't you start, too," she said, since she could feel another speech coming on. "I just had the day from hell, and frankly I've had enough."

"Did you remove Tex's garden gnomes?" Marge demanded, not deterred.

Immediately she turned a little weary. "Garden gnomes? I don't know nothing about no garden gnomes."

"They're all gone, and Tex is very upset."

"Well, I didn't take them," she said. "How could I have? I was at the office with Tex all day, and then I was over at the Star Hotel trying to save Jeff Morrison's life. Not that he was grateful, mind you. Instead, he went whining to Alec and Chase and told them some lie about me and Scarlett trying to murder him. As if we're a couple of vicious killers! Us! The people who have done more for this town than Alec himself!"

"Is Jeff all right?" asked Marge.

"He's fine," said Vesta. "He booked himself a room at the Star Hotel, since apparently he didn't like it here at the house. We're to send his stuff over to the hotel immediately."

"But why did he leave in the first place? Didn't he like his room?"

"Yeah, that must have been it. He probably didn't like the room."

"I should have known," said Marge. "Couldn't you have given me some advance notice that we had a guest staying here? I could have tidied up the room and made it look nice. Now it was almost as if we offered him the broom cupboard to stay in."

They ruminated on Jeff's sudden departure for a moment, then Vesta glanced outside, and saw that Marge wasn't lying.

All of Tex's gnomes were gone. Clearly Ted hadn't wasted any time getting rid of those eyesores.

Just then the doorbell rang, and she said, "Don't get up. I'll go."

"Thanks, ma," said Marge.

"No sweat." She unhurriedly traipsed along the hallway, and when she opened the door was surprised to see the same two idiots trying to sell her on some kind of bird tax before. Only this time they were both wearing funny-looking wigs and mustaches and were donning sunglasses.

"Mrs. Muffin," said the tallest of the two. He held up his fake IRS badge. "Are you aware of the new air tax the governor of our great state has issued? From now on, every pound of air a person consumes is being taxed. And judging from your height, weight, and age, the governor, in his eternal wisdom, has decided that your air tax amounts to one thousand five hundred dollars for this fiscal year, payable immediately."

She sighed. "Look, it's been a long day, fellas. So if you could please go and scam some other dope, I'd be very appreciative."

"Failure to comply will result in additional interest and penalties," the short one said.

"That's great, fella," she said. And since Chase had just pulled up in front of the house, she waved him over.

When the two men saw the cop towering over them and twiddling his handcuffs, they bowed their heads.

"How did you know it was us?" asked the tall one.

Clearly, these weren't criminal masterminds.

She returned indoors and wondered how she was going to break the news to Tex that his gnomes had suffered a fatal accident. After all, she had promised Ted that she would handle things on her end. But then she got a bright idea.

Even though the day had been long and taxing, it proved that her brain was still working at full capacity.

And so she took out her phone and placed the call.

* * *

AFTER ALL THE excitement of the chase at the Star Hotel, the four of us were glad to be home again, and as we entered the house, made a beeline for the couch, keen to enjoy a nice, long nap. Mostly it's crooks and killers that keep us up at night, but this time it had been our own human. But then I guess it's variety that is the spice of life, as the philosopher said. And we would have been sound asleep if Chase hadn't walked in, accompanied by Odelia, and started telling her all about the day he had had.

It involved a long and complicated lament about Gran, who wasn't his favorite person at that moment.

"Gran did what?" asked Odelia, who clearly couldn't believe her ears.

"And that's not all," said Chase. "After she chased that man through the hotel, stark-naked, if you please, she had the gall to demand that he arrange a date for her and Scarlett with two of his fellow doctors." He shook his head as he let himself drop down on the couch—our couch, I should add. "That woman is just too much."

"I don't know what's gotten into her all of a sudden," said Odelia.

"Old age," said Chase.

"No, she's been like this most of her life," said Odelia.

"It seems to be getting worse, though, doesn't it?"

"That poor Jeff," said Odelia. "Will he be pressing charges against Gran and Scarlett?"

"I don't think so," said Chase. "Alec tried to talk him out of it, and I think he was successful. He also told him that

Vesta didn't mean it like that. She thought she was doing a good thing last night by suggesting to Hannah Dunlop that she get rid of her husband's body."

"What's going to happen to Hannah now? And her sisters?"

"I think they'll be fine," said Chase. "From what I could tell, it really was an accident, so they're off the hook."

"Good," said Odelia. "If what Hannah said is true, Norbert wasn't a man but an animal. I can't imagine what that woman has had to suffer over the years."

"Yeah, I guess you never know what goes on in a marriage," said Chase. "Talking of marriages, have you seen your dad?"

"Not yet. I just got here."

"I was over next door just now, to arrest those weird scammers again, and he struck me as morose. According to your mom, someone has gone and stolen all of his gnomes."

Odelia smiled. "Are you sure it wasn't mom hiding them? She is not a big fan of those gnomes."

"Tex seems to think that Ted did it."

"Ted Trapper? He wouldn't."

"Well, if your dad wants to file a report against Ted, let me know. Though please make it tomorrow. I've had just about all the excitement I can stomach for one day. Did I tell you about that bank heist we handled today?"

And he proceeded to tell Odelia all about it, causing the four of us to reluctantly leave the house and look for a different place to lay our weary heads.

We ended up next door, but when we found Tex lamenting to Marge about his precious gnomes, we knew this wasn't the place to find some peace and quiet either. And so we moved on and found ourselves in the Trapper backyard, where a moody Rufus told us to make ourselves comfortable behind the garden house. After a while, I couldn't take it anymore, so I asked, "What's wrong, Rufus?"

"Ted won't play with me anymore," he said. "He even kicked my ball into the bushes when I asked him to play."

"That wasn't very nice of him," I said. And then I remembered how I had promised the sheepdog that Chase would play with him if Ted wouldn't.

"Why don't you head over to my backyard and offer your ball to Chase?" I suggested. "I'm sure he'd love to play with you."

He immediately perked up considerably. "Are you serious?"

"Absolutely. Go on, get that ball over there now, buddy."

"Oh, Max, you're such a good friend!" he cried, and off he went, on a trot, to offer his ball to the detective.

If I knew Chase, he would be more than happy to throw the ball around with the goofy floofball.

Finally, we had some peace and quiet to look forward to, and the four of us happily closed our eyes for some shuteye. Which is when suddenly an irate voice above our heads shouted, "So I give and give and give, but what do I get in return? Nada! Bupkis! Zilch!"

It was Stewart, and he did not look happy.

CHAPTER 31

When the cats came hurrying in to tell Vesta that she urgently had to feed the birds or else all hell would break loose, she groaned. As if she didn't have enough on her plate, now she had to risk getting caught by Marcie to keep her guano farm going.

"Can't they wait until after dark?" she lamented. "I mean, if I go over there with a bucket full of feed, Marcie will wonder what I'm up to. And I've seen her. She's home and she's on the prowl."

"Stewart says they haven't been fed all day," said Max. "And if they don't get fed now, the deal is off."

"All right, all right," she said, but then had a better idea. "I'll ask Ted to feed them. That way I don't have to pass by Marcie." And so she picked up her phone and put in a call to their neighbor Ted.

"Me!" Ted cried. "You actually expect me to feed those darn birds! They pooped on me, Vesta. They actually went and pooped on my head!"

"What were you doing in there in the first place, you nincompoop?" she asked.

"It's still my garden house," he said plaintively. "I can come and go as I please."

"Yeah, yeah, yeah. So can you feed them or not?"

"I cannot," he said, then suddenly lowered his voice. "I can't talk now. Marcie just walked in." And promptly the line went dead.

That was the trouble when you lived next door to the biggest gossip in all of Hampton Cove: you couldn't show your face or she had seen it, and you couldn't hold a decent conversation or she had heard it. And you couldn't feed your birds without risking discovery.

She plopped herself down on her chair and thought for a moment. There had to be a solution. She happened to glance down at her cats and saw that all four of them were looking at her expectantly, and then she had it.

"You're going to feed those birds," she told them.

"Us!" Brutus cried. "But we don't know the first thing about feeding birds."

"How hard can it be? You just take some feed and give it to them. Problem solved." She got up and walked into the pantry where she kept the bag of bird feed she had picked up from Wilbur. "Look here," she said. "Take some of this stuff into your mouths, sneak over there, and drop it in the trough I've installed. Can you do that for me?"

The cats didn't look happy about it, but since she didn't leave them much of a choice, in the end it was decided. And since she figured they might as well do it the way it should be done, she installed herself on her side of the hedge with a bucket of bird feed and watched as the cats took some of it in their mouths and then walked to the other side.

"And don't swallow!" she cried when Dooley tentatively picked up some of the stuff.

He shook his head and said, "I won't, Gran," causing all of the feed to fall from his mouth again.

"And don't talk," she said as she gave him a pat on the head. "There's a good boy."

She watched as they took off in the direction of the garden shed and entered, their mouths full of feed, and came out without. Excellent work. Now let Alec tell her again what an idiot she was. She was probably the cleverest thinking person on planet Earth, maybe the entire universe.

It only took them a couple of trips to empty that bucket and provide the birds with the food they needed. And then later tonight, when the biggest gossip in town was fast asleep to give her mouth some much-needed rest, she would sneak over there herself with a bag of the stuff and fill that trough up nice and proper and harvest some more of that precious guano.

"How much guano is there already?" she asked when Max returned from his sixth trip.

The big orange cat spat out a couple of seeds and shrugged. "The stuff is all over the place, Gran. They've really been busy, those birds. Though Stewart says they're getting antsy and restless. I guess you can't keep those birds in there for too long before they want to fly the nest. They are birds, after all, and hate to be locked up all the time."

"I don't care," she said. "They're working for me now, and they should do as I say." After all, she was the one feeding them and offering them a nice place to stay. "And besides, I made a deal with Stewart, and as long as I keep up my side of the bargain, I expect him to keep his. You tell him, Max."

Max sighed. "All right, Gran. I'll tell him." And he scooped up another nice helping of seed into his mouth and was off. Good little helpers, she thought. That's how it should be. Everybody doing as they were told.

Just then, her phone chimed and when she took it out of her pocket she saw that it was Wilbur. Another good little helper, this time of the watch. "Well? Did you get me what I need?"

"I did," said the shopkeeper. "But it wasn't easy to get it in the quantities that you want. Are you sure this is all legal and above board?"

"Are you kidding me? I'm the leader of the watch, Wilbur. As a rule, everything I do is always legal and above board, even if it isn't. Now when are you going to bring it over?"

"How about tonight? I have to be careful not to spill any, though. This stuff is extremely corrosive." He paused. "What are you planning to do with it anyway?"

"None of your business," she said. "Oh, and when you bring it, don't park in front of the house, will you? Go around the back."

"You mean park in Blake's Field?"

"That's exactly right."

"Okay, fine. But I want no part of this, you hear me?"

"No part of what? You don't even know what I'm going to use it for."

"Exactly, and I'd like to keep it that way." And with these words, he disconnected. She tapped the phone against her teeth. If Wilbur was to deliver the stuff via Blake's Field, she would need another helping hand to transfer it from his van to the fence. Good thing she was the leader of the watch and had plenty of helping hands on standby.

Which is why she engaged Scarlett and Francis in a conference call and told them to be present at the house that night.

"Are we going on a mission?" asked Scarlett.

"That's right. A very exciting mission."

"I love a nice mission," said Francis. "I just hope there are no dead bodies involved this time. All that excitement last night didn't do my ticker any favors. I've had heart palpitations all day just thinking about poor Norbert."

"Poor Norbert was a wife beater," she reminded him.

"All the same. He didn't deserve to die like that. But I've been praying for his soul and I feel much better now."

"This mission, it isn't anything to do with your guano farm, is it, Vesta?" asked Scarlett. When Vesta kept mum, she added, "What are you going to do with all those millions?"

"Invest them in the watch, of course—what else?"

"Do you mean that?"

"Absolutely. I'm all for making Hampton Cove a safer place, honey, you know that. And if we had the funds, we could finally get a decent set of wheels and some of that snazzy equipment."

"I'm all for a decent set of wheels," said Francis. "So let's sell some of that delicious guano and bring the watch into the twenty-first century. And maybe we can keep some of it for ourselves, to celebrate when we buy the car. On a scale of one to ten, how tasty is it, this guano?"

"Guano isn't something you can eat, Francis," she said.

"It isn't? But I thought it was an Italian delicacy?"

"It's bird poop. You spread it on the field like manure."

"And here I thought you spread it on your pasta."

"You could, but it would probably ruin the pasta."

And with these words, they ended the call.

Tonight was going to be one heck of a night.

She could feel it in her aged bones.

CHAPTER 32

Evening had come, and the four of us were getting ready to leave for cat choir when we saw some suspicious activity in Blake's Field. Brutus was the first one to alert us of this when he jumped on the back fence and spotted some suspicious figures moving about back there.

"We better check this out, you guys," he said when he came to fetch us.

Dooley and I had just partaken in our humans' meal—or at least some of the remnants of it—and had eaten our fill to the bursting point, which probably is never a good idea. Then again, how can one resist a piece of actual lamb fricassee? And since Marge had made too much, she decided to dispense with the surplus portion to her cats. Even Harriet had eaten more than she should have and was asking Marge to provide her with some tips on how to keep her perfect and enviable slim size. Brutus had eaten so much he felt he needed to walk it off, which is how he had come to spot those mysterious figures moving about in the field behind our house.

"I'll bet it's those scammers again," said Harriet. "Chase

keeps arresting them, and they keep getting released by the judge and returning to scam more people."

"But how come the judge releases them?" asked Dooley. "Shouldn't they be in prison where they belong?"

Harriet shrugged. "The judge's ways are mysterious. We all know that."

"So are you coming or what?" asked Brutus, getting impatient. "They'll be gone soon!"

And so we hurried out of the house after our friend, though I should probably add that I was finding it quite impossible to do a lot of hurrying since my stomach was preventing me from doing so. Instead, I walked along at a gait a touch more vigorous than usual, all the while wondering if I had overdone things to such an extent I'd have to lie down for a couple of hours.

Jumping the fence was a big no-no in my condition, and the same could be said about Harriet and Dooley. Even Brutus, notoriously a muscular kind of cat, found it hard going. And so instead, we slipped into Kurt's backyard and used the tunnel that Fifi has made there, which leads under the fence.

Our neighbor was curious about what we were up to, so we told her about the mysterious and suspicious activities, leading her to immediately get all excited and follow us on our adventure. I could have told her that I planned to stay far away from these mysterious figures since I didn't want to spoil my dinner, but then Fifi is one of those remarkably active dogs. Perhaps I would even use the word hyperactive, but never when she can hear me.

It wasn't long before we arrived at the scene of the crime in progress—if indeed a crime was being committed. Much to our surprise, it wasn't a gang of hardened criminals hard at work to wreak havoc on our neighborhood, but the neighborhood watch!

"Gran!" said Dooley when we came across our very own human, accompanied by Scarlett, Wilbur, and Father Reilly. "What are you doing?"

"Oh, this and that," said our human vaguely. "Shouldn't you be at cat choir at this hour?"

"Brutus had noticed some suspicious activity, so we wanted to check it out," said Dooley.

I saw that the watch had acquired an extra member in the form of Benny, the ex-con who had been so helpful last night in endeavoring to cut up Norbert's body.

"I hope he won't be cutting people up tonight," said Harriet with a look of distaste as she gestured to the butcher.

"He won't," said Gran curtly. "And now you better get going. You don't want to be late for your recital, do you?"

And she actually ushered us off!

"Why do I get the feeling that Gran is trying to get rid of us?" asked Dooley.

"Because she is," I said.

And since cats are very hard to get rid of, we decided not to follow Gran's urgings but instead double back and spy on her and the other members of the watch. If she was up to something, we had a right to know. This was our neighborhood. And we might not officially be members of the watch, but we formed a kind of watch of our own: the cat watch. Okay, so maybe I should say the pet watch, since we featured one dog in our midst in the form of Fifi.

"Do you think they're going to try and get rid of Norbert again?" asked Dooley.

"No, according to Chase, Norbert is at the morgue," I said.

"Maybe they took his body from the morgue to make him disappear?" my friend suggested.

"Now what would be the point of that?"

He thought hard about this but couldn't find a solution,

PURRFECT GRAN

proving I was probably right and that whatever Gran and her friends were up to was unrelated to last night's events.

Wilbur had backed a flatbed truck all the way up to the fence that divided this part of the field from Tex and Marge's backyard, and as we watched on, the four members of the watch, along with Benny, started unloading something from the bed of the truck. It was a metal drum, just like the one we had seen in the alley behind the Star that day.

"Another drum," said Brutus. "What is going on?"

"Maybe it's the same drum?" Harriet suggested.

"But why would they bring it all the way out here?" I asked.

"Rainwater is good for the plants, Max," said Harriet. "Everyone knows that. So maybe they want to water the plants?"

"I very much doubt that the neighborhood watch would get involved in something as mundane as that," I said. "They're in the crime prevention business, not the plant watering business."

"Careful!" Wilbur yelled as Benny almost tripped and fell, dragging the drum down with him. "If this thing spills all over you, that will be the end for you, buddy boy."

"Don't get your panties in a wad, old man," said Benny, who was chewing a piece of gum, I saw, and looking very pleased with himself. "Where do you want this, Vesta?"

"Put it over there," said Vesta, pointing to a spot right next to the fence.

"I have to say I still don't feel entirely at ease about this scheme of yours, Vesta," said Father Reilly. "Are you sure this guano will fetch us as much as you say it will?"

"More," said Gran as she oversaw the proceedings. "Put it down, boys. I think we did it."

"How do you open it?" asked Scarlett.

"Very carefully," said Wilbur, who didn't look entirely at

ease either. "If only a drop of this spills on any of you, I'll be in big trouble."

"You know, Father," said Benny as he stepped back from the drum, satisfied with a job well done, "I really enjoy this whole rehabilitation project you've got going for me. I never knew that civilian life could be this exciting."

"That's exactly why I've asked you to help us out on these little projects of ours," said the priest. "To make you see that civilian life doesn't have to be boring. It's all about being of service, young Benny. Being of service and caring for your community."

"Oh, I love being of service," said the kid. "It's the life for me, all right." He rubbed his hands. "So who goes in first?"

"It's not who goes in first," Francis corrected him gently. "But what goes in first." He directed a questioning look at Vesta. "Are you ready?"

Vesta nodded, and as she dragged a tarp up from a hidden place next to the fence, great was our surprise when that tarp turned out to be covering dozens of gnomes. And if I wasn't mistaken, they were all Tex's gnomes! Some of them had been broken into little pieces, almost as if someone had taken a hammer to them.

"What is Gran doing with those gnomes?" asked Dooley.

"I have a feeling she's going to make them disappear," I said.

"But why? Doesn't she know how fond Tex is of his gnomes?"

"These are some strange goings-on," said Fifi, but I could see that she was loving every minute of this adventure we were having. "I just wish that Rufus was here." Then she got a bright idea. "Why don't I go and fetch him?"

And before we could stop her, she was off at a happy trot, to fetch her friend. We watched her go with a baleful eye since Rufus isn't the kind of dog who can come and go undetected. He's big and fluffy and, most of all, noisy. But then since Fifi was already gone, there was nothing we could do about it.

"Okay, so how do we do this?" asked Vesta.

"Just chuck 'em in," said Wilbur. "But careful—very careful! One drop of this stuff and—"

"There will be hell to pay. I know, I know," said Gran as she picked up one of Tex's garden gnomes and held it up next to the drum. Then, ever so carefully, she tipped it in.

Five humans stood around the drum, watching the gnome disappear into whatever the drum contained. And judging from their response, I had a feeling that this time it wasn't rainwater!

"Amazing," said Scarlett. "It's gone already."

"Vanished into thin air," said Father Reilly.

"I told you this stuff was pretty amazing," said Wilbur proudly. "You can't beat sulfuric acid!"

"Where did it go?" asked Gran. "I don't get it."

"It dissolved," Benny explained, still chewing energetically. "You should see what it can do with a human body. Though it takes a little more time to dissolve the bones, of course. And the teeth. And the skull. But eventually, it takes care of the whole person. Skin, flesh, bones, hair, teeth—the whole lot of it. Just like Drano." He looked around excitedly. "Are you sure we can't get that fat dude from last night and chuck him in?"

"Now, now, Benny," said Father Reilly, clapping him gently on the shoulder.

"I'm sorry," said Benny. "I guess I get carried away, you know. The prison shrink always said I loved my job too much, and that was part of the problem."

"That's all right. Instead of getting rid of people, you can get rid of gnomes now," said Father Reilly.

Judging from Benny's expression, he seemed to feel it

wasn't exactly the same thing. Then again, killing gnomes probably carries a much lighter sentence than killing a human being, so Father Reilly had a point.

"Okay, so let's do this, folks," said Gran. "Each take a gnome and dump it in. There's a whole pile to get through, so let's not waste time, all right?"

And so the five members of the Gnome Removal Squad started feeding those unfortunate gnomes to the drum filled with sulfuric acid and making sure they would never be seen again. It certainly gave new meaning to the term 'sleep with the fishes.' There were no fishes here, of course, and gnomes aren't people. Still, I had a feeling that if Tex knew, he wouldn't be too pleased that his mother-in-law was dissolving his precious gnomes in acid with the assistance of the entire neighborhood watch.

And they had been going well when all of a sudden a head popped up over the fence. It wasn't Tex, though, but Marcie Trapper. And as she surveyed the scene, it wasn't long before she was detected.

"Marcie!" Scarlett cried, giving Gran a nudge with her elbow. "How nice to see you here!"

"I wanted to ask you a favor," said Marcie.

"What favor?" asked Gran irritably. "We're already getting rid of Tex's gnomes for you. What more do you want in exchange for letting us use that garden house of yours?"

"How many gnomes can that stuff take?" asked Marcie.

All eyes turned to Benny, the resident expert on all things sulfuric acid. He shifted his chewing gum to the other side of his mouth and considered the question carefully. "I once fed three guys to a bathtub filled with sulfuric acid," he said. "But I have to add that they were small fellas. Chinese mobsters. Tiny little dudes. How many gnomes are we talking here, Mrs..."

"Trapper," said Marcie. She thought for a moment. "I

PURRFECT GRAN

think Ted has about a hundred now? Something like that? I'm not sure. He keeps buying new ones all the time. And frankly, I'm sick and tired of it. I can't put one foot down without stepping on one of those hideous creatures. I want them gone, Vesta. I want them all gone—every last one of them."

Vesta shared a look with Scarlett, and the latter nodded.

"Okay, fine," said Gran. "Hand them over the fence, and we'll feed them to the acid."

"I can't do this alone," said Marcie. "You'll have to help me collect them. Like I said, there are at least a hundred of these things."

"We'll hop over the fence, no problem," said Benny.

"Let's organize this," Father Reilly suggested. "One person needs to be on this side of the fence to take delivery of the gnomes, one person has to lower them into the acid, so…" He quickly did a head count. "There's six of us here, so four people should be on the other side of the fence. Who wants to help Marcie collect the gnomes?" He immediately stuck up his hand, and so did Scarlett and Gran. And so it was decided: Wilbur and Benny would take care of gnome destruction while the other four would be on the hunter-gatherer team, rounding up every last gnome.

But then a thought occurred to Wilbur. "Won't Ted mind?" he asked all of a sudden.

"Of course he will mind," said Marcie. "But he won't know that we got rid of his gnomes, will he?"

"He's out, is he, your husband?" asked Father Reilly.

"Yeah, he's gone to a team-building night with his work colleagues. They're going bowling, and judging from last year's experience, he won't be back before midnight, so that should give us plenty of time to do this."

Which is how the strangest sight played out before our very eyes: a sort of conga line was formed with gnomes being passed over the fence and doused in acid, making sure Marcie was finally rid of the pint-sized bearded freaks.

Dooley turned to me, a look of stupefaction on his face. "Max," he said. "Just when you think you've seen it all, something like this happens!"

CHAPTER 33

Ted Trapper wasn't feeling well. A stomach bug, most likely. Which was inconvenient for this was the night that he and his colleagues had arranged to enjoy their annual game of bowling. Officially it had been entered on the calendar as a team-building night, but mostly it was simply an opportunity to gossip about management and to have some fun. But no matter how much he enjoyed these outings, his tummy was playing up so badly he didn't think he could go on. And so halfway into the proceedings, he announced to his team members that he was going home.

Oddly enough, they weren't exactly falling over themselves to convince him to stay, though the fact that his team was losing badly might have had something to do with that. It was true that he wasn't exactly a gifted bowler, and he often got picked last when the teams were formed—high school football all over again.

He parked his car in front of the house and got out, satisfied that the lights were still on inside, a sign that Marcie was still up. He'd take something for his stomach, and they could sit and watch something on TV until it was time to go to bed.

Only when he entered the living room, of Marcie, there was no trace. And when he looked for her upstairs, she wasn't there either. She wasn't in the kitchen. She wasn't in the basement. Where was she?

And it was as he stood scratching his head and staring out of the kitchen window that he saw several people, one of whom was his wife, collecting his gnomes and taking them to the fence, only to pop them over!

What the heck!

He hurried outside and reached Marcie just when the final gnome made the journey over the fence!

"Honey!" he cried. "What are you doing!"

Marcie gave him one of those steely looks he knew so well. She had perfected that look when their girls had hit puberty and had started dating a series of highly unsuitable boys. Marcie had put the fear of God into so many pimple-faced hormonal teenagers that Ted had lost count.

"I hate those gnomes of yours, Ted," she said, much to his surprise. "I've always hated them, but lately, I hate them even more. The more you collect, the more I hate them!"

"But honey, why didn't you say so?"

"You spend so much money on those stupid things—money you could be spending on a nice cruise, or that trip to Europe you have been promising me. Or a second honeymoon. But no! It has to be another expensive gnome!"

"They're not that expensive," he argued, but it was obvious from Marcie's death-ray glare that he'd better shut up right now if he still wanted to stay married to the woman.

"So... what's going to happen to them?" he asked, gesturing to Francis Reilly, Vesta Muffin, and Scarlett Canyon, who were Marcie's accomplices in this gnome-removal operation. "Are you putting them in storage somewhere? Or are you going to sell them?"

Marcie gave him a cruel smile, a smile he had never seen

on his wife's face before. If he didn't know any better, he would have said that it was the smile of a serial killer.

"The gnomes are no more, Ted. No more, you hear me?"

"What do you mean, the gnomes are no more?" It seemed like an odd thing to say.

"Never again will they darken our doorstep."

And with these mysterious words, she turned away from him and joined Vesta, Scarlett, and Francis as they used his ladder to scale the fence. His curiosity aroused, he followed them, and that's when he got the shock of a lifetime.

On the other side of the fence, a liquid was bubbling in a large drum, while Wilbur Vickery and a man he had never seen before fed his precious gnomes into the liquid. And as he watched, the goofy little tykes simply… vanished!

It was possibly the most horrific thing he had ever witnessed in his entire life.

* * *

JEFF MORRISON HAD BEEN THINKING HARD about what Chief Lip and Detective Kingsley had told him that morning. According to Chief Lip, Vesta Muffin wasn't the dangerous psychopath he had her pegged as. She was a pain in the patootie, that was true, and more trouble than she was worth. The Chief had told Jeff a couple of anecdotes about the stunts Vesta had pulled in her day, and each time the fallout had been for her son to clean up. But she wasn't dangerous—not dangerous at all. And so he shouldn't have been afraid that she was going to do something to him.

Granted, her initiative to help her neighbor Hannah get rid of her husband's body was ill-advised at best, but it had come from a good place: to want to help a friend and neighbor. And so Jeff should rest assured: she never would have caused him any harm.

It had certainly given him a lot to think about. And so he had finally decided that maybe he had been a little rash in his reaction after Vesta and Scarlett had chased him last night, and also chased him through the hotel that day. Maybe it had all been one big misunderstanding, just as Chief Lip and the detective had told him.

And as he thought things through, he felt terrible. Marge Poole had opened her home for him and how had he repaid her? By running away and booking a room at the Star. What must she think of him? How ungrateful must she feel he had been? And it was this sentiment, more than anything, that set him on a quest to make amends. To apologize to Marge and Tex Poole and explain to them the reasoning behind his actions. He also wanted to apologize to Vesta, for he now felt he had been extremely rude to her.

And so he had instructed a cab to take him to Harrington Street, where he now stood poised with his finger on the buzzer, hoping to find the lady of the house at home and susceptible to his heartfelt apology. Oddly enough, there was no response, even though he could clearly see that the Pooles were home, since the lights were on.

The only thing he could think was that they were out back and couldn't hear the bell. And so it was with a pep in his step that he walked around the house and headed to the back where he hoped to find Marge and Tex and the rest of the family. He had even brought along a bouquet of roses for Marge and a bottle of wine from the Star store for Tex. That should make them more amenable to forgiving him for his terrible behavior.

When he arrived at the back of the house, to his surprise, he didn't find the Pooles there either. What he did hear was the sound of people arguing. And since he was essentially a curious man, he walked over to the fence to see what was going on. Standing on his tiptoes to peek over, he was surprised to find the same man who had threatened to cut him up into little pieces and make his body disappear in a drum of acid on the other side. And as their eyes met, the killer's eyes narrowed and a cruel smile slid up his face.

"Well, look who's here!" said the freak.

And as Jeff glanced past the psycho killer, he saw a large drum filled with bubbling liquid. Something was floating on top that could only be part of a human being. And surrounding the drum stood the entire Poole clan, Chief Lip and Detective Kingsley included. The moment they became aware of his presence, they all stared at him with what can only be termed murderous intent. The cold looks of a gang of vicious killers!

Which is why he ran away from the scene screaming. The moment he entered the cab, he told the cabbie to take him as far from Hampton Cove as fast as humanly possible. It was clear now that Chief Lip had been lying, and also Detective Kingsley. And the reason was obvious: they were both part of the gang!

Never would he set foot in this Stepford town again!

CHAPTER 34

Things were getting a little out of control, I felt, with first Tex and Marge coming upon the scene, after having become curious by all the noise and activity next door, and then of course, Odelia and Chase had also arrived. And even Uncle Alec, when one of the neighbors phoned the police to alert them of strange goings-on in Blake's Field, assuming that burglars were targeting their homes.

Tex wasn't happy when he discovered that his gnomes had all been dissolved in acid, and even though Marge didn't seem to mind very much—like Marcie, she had never been a big fan of her husband's hobby—she still showed him the necessary support when confronted with the demise of his beloved terracotta creatures.

I saw that she had sidled up to Marcie, though, when Tex wasn't looking, and the two women bumped fists and shared a happy smile that their shared ordeal was finally over now. Though I could have told them that obsessives like Tex and Ted aren't deterred by a minor setback like this, and that very soon they would be raiding garden centers all across the state to return their collections to their former glory.

I could see it in Tex's face, and also Ted's. They might even start pooling their resources from now on—which would be bad news for their respective spouses.

Luckily for the latter, Wilbur presumably had more sulfuric acid ready if such a contingency should occur. In the end, I now saw, the real gnome war wasn't between Tex and Ted but between those two and their respective wives. And I had a good idea of who would win.

"Uncle Alec looks unhappy, Max," said Dooley.

"Yeah, he doesn't seem to appreciate the watch's latest mission," I agreed.

"I think Gran was right to get rid of the gnomes," said Harriet. She raised her head. "I've never liked those horrid creatures. They smell foul, for one thing, and they are freaky. Just the way they look at you gives me the creeps. And don't even get me started on those beards." She shivered, and I could fully sympathize, as Tex's hobby has always left me cold as well.

"Do you think Gran is in trouble now?" asked Dooley.

"I'll bet she isn't," said Brutus. "There's no law against destroying your own gnomes, is there? And after all, Marcie was the instigator in this instance, so technically speaking this is a matter between husband and wife and not the concern of the strong hand of the law."

"Yes, but what about Tex's gnomes?"

"Again, strictly a family matter," said Brutus, who had given this matter some thought. "Gran took her son-in-law's gnomes and recycled them." He shrugged. "I don't see the problem."

Tex did see the problem, though. Or better yet, he didn't see it, since the gnomes had been eradicated. Wiped from the face of the planet. Zapped in one fell swoop.

"I really like this sulfuric acid," said Dooley. "It's a very clean solution, isn't it? You can feed it anything and it simply disappears. I really don't know how it does it, but it certainly does it well."

"Very efficient," I agreed.

"Maybe there's some more stuff we should feed into that drum while we have the chance?" Dooley suggested.

"Like what?" asked Brutus.

"Oh, I know," said Harriet. "Some of Gran's shoes are truly hideous, and also some of those tracksuits she insists on wearing. I would get rid of all of them. And of course, that gym equipment that Chase has installed in the guest bedroom. I keep bumping against it and I think Odelia wouldn't mind if we got rid of that, too."

"I'm not sure metal dissolves in acid," I said thoughtfully.

"We could give it a try," Harriet suggested. And before we could stop her, she was approaching Odelia to make the suggestion to her in person. I could see our human's eyes sparkle when she heard Harriet's words, and her fingers were itching to make them a reality. But then she glanced over to Chase, and I guess she didn't think it was worth antagonizing her husband about.

A marriage is very much like a democracy: a lot of different political parties, all fighting like cats and dogs, but in the end, they still have a country to run and have to get along somehow. So they compromise, just like Odelia was doing now. And just like Marge and Marcie had been doing all these years. Though clearly sometimes you also have to take a stand when things get out of hand, like with the gnome sitch.

One man also seemed to see the endless possibilities that opened up now that we had a drum of acid in our midst, and that man was Benny. I could see his hands twitching to lay them on certain persons and make them disappear forever. Perhaps his former associates, or the people who had ratted him out and got him locked up in prison. Or the judge who had sentenced him. Or the lawyer who hadn't pleaded his case as he should have. Or some of his fellow inmates. But Chase was also aware of this, and kept a close eye on the man, and so did Father Reilly. He was, after all, responsible for the man's spiritual rehabilitation and wasn't going to allow him to stray from the straight and narrow. Except when it was a matter of making the body of an annoying neighbor and bad husband disappear, or a couple of gnomes.

And just when I thought that things had calmed down considerably, and a truce had been reached between the different parties involved in the fracas, a new face arrived at the scene, or rather popped up over the fence. It was Jeff, and as the doctor took in the scene, I could tell that he was horrified, shocked, and dismayed.

He took one look at the drum filled with acid, where several members of the gnome family were still bubbling away, resigned to their fate, and then at the people gathered around the drum, uttered a sort of loud shriek of terror and was off like a bat out of hell.

I think the whole neighborhood must have heard him. Moments later a car backfired and took off at a high rate of speed.

"I think Jeff is leaving town," Brutus remarked.

"Yeah, I have a feeling we won't be seeing him again," I said.

"Too bad," said Harriet. "I liked him. And it's always good to have a brain surgeon on standby. You never know when you might need one."

With a family filled with crazy people, she was probably right. Then again, the Pooles might be crazy, but they're not dangerous. Also, they're kind to pets and babies, so there's that.

CHAPTER 35

Because he was so upset about the demise of his gnomes, Tex had decided that he wouldn't officiate as the grillmaster for the family's feast, and so Uncle Alec and Chase had been forced to take over that important task—though I have to say I saw several faces light up with delight at the doctor's announcement, having more faith in the new chefs' skills. Tex has improved considerably over the course of the last couple of years as a chef, but judging from the response his decision garnered, he still has a long way to go.

I guess cats aren't as choosy as humans are. Because for me, Tex did a pretty good job. But then I'm not a gourmet, per se.

But even though Tex had also threatened not to attend the feast, and to boycott the shindig over his disapproval of Gran's role in the affair, in the end he had decided that would be taking things too far. And so he was there, but his face registered dismay, and he had decided to stay as far away from his mother-in-law as possible, and also not to talk to her anymore. Something that Gran didn't seem at all bothered with.

"I wonder how they're going to handle work at the practice now," said Harriet. "It can't be easy for Tex to have a receptionist he has sworn not to talk to anymore."

"Maybe he'll give her little notes?" Brutus suggested.

"Or maybe he'll fire Gran and hire Scarlett," said Harriet. "He has done it before, remember?"

I did remember, and it hadn't been neither Gran nor Scarlett's finest hour, as their acrimony had turned physical at some point, with echoes of the big Krystle Carrington and Alexis Colby fight. It had been back when they didn't get along and had declared themselves to be mortal enemies. Which just goes to show how quickly things can change. Even Ted and Tex were friends now, united in their grief, and so were Marge and Marcie, united in their victory.

"So what's going to happen to Gran's guano farm?" asked Brutus.

"I'm not sure," I said. Though my best guess was that it was still running at full capacity, with Stewart and his friends giving of their best, or rather, their poop.

"Imagine that our poop would be worth its weight in gold," said Harriet. "Now wouldn't that be something?"

"I'm sure our poop is valuable," said Brutus. "I mean, poop is poop, after all, and farmers will be happy to have it and throw it on their fields."

"No, but there's something very special about bird poop," said Dooley. "Gran has been doing a lot of research into the matter, and she says not all poop is equal. Otherwise, she could harvest her own poop and sell that to Farmer Giles."

We all shared a look of surprise. "Imagine Gran collecting her own poop," said Harriet. "That wouldn't be very pleasant, would it? I mean, how would she even go about it?"

"She would probably have to use a receptacle of some

kind," I said. "And then collect the stuff and leave it to dry, maybe?"

Uncle Alec and Chase had finished the preparatory stages of their work, and Odelia now handed us our dinner on a platter—not a silver one, but that was fine with me. I'm not too hung up on etiquette. We all tucked in, and soon only the sounds of four cats eating were heard, against the backdrop of our humans' pleasant conversation—except Tex, of course, who had taken a vow of silence, it would seem.

We hadn't even finished yet when Rufus suddenly came bursting into our backyard. "You guys!" he said. "It's the birds! They're mounting an uprising!"

And since this was something we needed to see with our own eyes, we jumped off the porch swing and followed our friend into his own backyard. When we arrived there, we saw that Fifi was also in attendance, and she actually looked scared.

"The birds have gone completely mad!" she cried.

And as we watched where she was pointing, I saw that she was right: the birds had all escaped the garden house and were circling the structure, flocking to it and moving away in waves, almost as if they were ready to go on the attack.

"What's got them so worked up?" asked Brutus as we watched the eerie scene.

"No idea," said Rufus. "They were fine this morning, but after your gran paid them a visit to throw more feed into their trough and scoop their poop, they got very restless, and now it seems as if they're ready to launch into some kind of retaliatory campaign."

Brutus gave me a gentle nudge. "You're our spokesperson, Max," he said. "You better go over there and talk to the bird in charge."

"I'm not sure I'm the right person to…"

But Brutus and Harriet both gave me a shove in the direction of the garden house.

"Oh, okay, so this is happening," I said, and moved off to talk to the birds. When I saw that Dooley was right behind me, I said, "Maybe you better stay back, buddy."

"I'm not leaving your side, Max," he said, though I could sense that he wasn't at ease either. The birds did look extremely agitated, I thought, screaming and screeching up a storm.

We found Stewart seated on top of the garden house, and when we approached, he gave us an unfriendly look.

"Your human betrayed us," he declared immediately.

"What did she do?" I asked, casting a nervous look at the rest of his flock.

"She said she was going to feed us some prime feed, but instead, she's been giving us the worst stuff I've ever tasted. Clearly she figured we wouldn't notice the difference, but we do. And so we've decided that if she doesn't feel the need to keep up her side of the bargain, we don't need to keep up ours."

"But… you promised," I said.

"And we are going to deliver," said Stewart. "But we never said how we would deliver and where," he added with a smirk, and before I could respond, he fluttered up and joined the rest of the flock, and they were off in the direction of the next backyard—our backyard!

And as the sounds of humans screaming and yelling reached my ears, I had a good idea of what must have happened.

The flock passed on, and as we all hurried back next door, I saw that all of our humans were covered in bird excrement, and so was all of the food, the grill, the table, and pretty much every possible surface.

"This is all your doing!" Uncle Alec cried as he rose to his feet. He had a nice big splash of bird poop on top of his head, and he didn't seem to like it.

"What are you complaining about?" said Gran. "Maybe it will get your hair growing again."

Oddly enough, she didn't have one bit of poo on her, but then I guess Gran is one of those people who always escapes the consequences of her own actions, much to her family's chagrin.

"Our guano!" said Scarlett. "Our precious guano!"

Charlene scooped a piece of poop from her face. "What are you talking about? This isn't guano. Guano is bat poop, and this is regular bird poop."

Gran looked disappointed. "You mean this isn't liquid gold?"

"Are you kidding me? Of course not. It's just shit, woman! Bird shit!"

"So... it isn't worth its weight in gold?"

The mayor scoffed. "It's worth nothing! Nothing!" And she stomped off for the house to get cleaned up, quickly followed by the rest of the clan. Finally only Gran and Scarlett remained. They shared a look.

"I still think it must be worth something," said Gran, ever the optimist.

"Yeah, Charlene was simply annoyed that her nice dress got some of that guano on it," said Scarlett.

"I could have told her that it will do wonders for her complexion," said Gran. "It might even get rid of those crow's feet she's got. She didn't have those before, did she? Must be living with Alec that's causing her to age prematurely."

Scarlett scooped up some of the poop from the roast beef. "Should I give it a try, you think?"

"Absolutely. It's the perfect beauty serum. Rub some of that stuff on your face for a couple of days and your skin will look like a baby's bottom."

"I'm a baby," Grace suddenly piped up. She had come crawling from underneath the table where she had been hiding. "So technically my bottom is like a baby's bottom. So what happens when I rub that stuff on me?"

"You'll disappear," Harriet quipped. And as we all watched on, both Scarlett and Gran actually did rub the bird poop on their faces.

"Soon we'll look young again," said Scarlett happily.

"Maybe we could market this stuff?" Gran suggested. Dollar signs had appeared in her eyes. "We could build a beauty empire, just like Kylie Jenner, and become billionaires." She held up the poop. "And then when we're interviewed by Forbes, we can declare that it all started with a bird named Stewart. Our own origin story."

At that moment, Stewart returned. His resentment must have run deep, for he released another salvo, this time landing right on top of the leader of the neighborhood watch and her second-in-command.

"That's what you get for taking me for a fool!" Stewart cried, and then fluttered off, but not before casting a final contemptuous look down at those mere mortals below.

"Stewart, come back!" Gran yelled. "You need to help us build our billion-dollar beauty empire! Stewart!"

"Guano!" Scarlett cried. "We need your guano!" But Stewart was gone, taking all of his precious guano—or non-guano, according to Charlene—along with him. He was like the bird that passed on with his song still unsung, or in this case his shit unshat.

"Looks like Gran won't be a billionaire, Max," said Dooley.

"Yeah, I got that same feeling," I said.

We hopped back onto our porch swing, which, because it was located underneath the porch, hadn't been hit by the birds' salvo, and was still as clean as before.

NIC SAINT

"I wonder why Gran doesn't smear cat poop on her face," Dooley began, but we all quickly shut him up. The last thing we needed was to put strange ideas into Gran's head. It was bad enough as it was without her locking us up in Ted's garden shed and turning us into poop-producing battery cats. She might do it, too.

Instead, we put our heads down and waited for our humans to return from the bathroom to resume the feast. Hopefully, they would clean up the grill and get busy cooking some fine morsels of meat again. Before long, we had all fallen asleep. It had been a pretty challenging couple of days, after all. For a moment there we had thought that Gran had become a murderer, but then in the end it had proven not to be the case. She might be batty, but not *that* batty.

"Max?" asked Dooley.

"Mh?" I said without opening my eyes.

"Do you think we should smear guano on our faces?"

"No, Dooley, I don't think we should do that," I said.

"For one thing, our faces are covered in fur," Harriet pointed out. "So if we do get wrinkles, they won't be noticeable. And for another…" Her head suddenly came up. "Dooley, you may be on to something."

"I am?" asked Dooley, well pleased.

"What if we smear that stuff on our fur? It might make it shinier!"

"Your fur is shiny enough, babes," said Brutus as he lazily opened one eye.

She gave him a haughty look. "Honey poo, there is no such thing as fur that is shiny enough."

We watched in amazement as she hopped down from the swing, high-tailed it over to the nearest patch of bird poop, and applied some of it to her fur.

"Baby, what are you doing!" Brutus cried.

"Making myself even more beautiful than I already am," she said as she pranced around a little. "I know, it's almost impossible to imagine such a thing, but you have to set the bar high, which is what I'm doing now." She thought for a moment, then shrugged, and actually went and rolled around in the stuff!

"But sugar plum!" Brutus cried as he grasped his head. "You are not a pig, why do you roll around in that muck!"

"Have you ever seen a pig with wrinkles?" she asked. "Well, that should tell you all you need to know."

Gran, who had been watching with amazement, snapped her fingers. "I know what we should do. Start a cosmetics line for cats! It's a gap in the market!"

"Vesta, you're brilliant!" Scarlett cried. "That's genius!"

And so both Scarlett and Gran got busy snapping pictures of Scarlett, who happily posed for the wannabe cosmetics giants.

All in all, it could have been worse: they could have asked the rest of us to also roll around in that stuff and pose for an impromptu photo shoot. And as the idea struck me, it also struck Brutus and Dooley. We shared a look of anguish and then found ourselves hurrying from the scene as fast as our legs could carry us.

"Hey, where are you going!" Gran cried. "I need you for the photo shoot! Max, roll around in this stuff for me, will you? Max! Dooley, come back here! Brutus—come back right now! I'm going to make you famous, all four of you!"

As we hurried off, two men appeared on the scene. One was short and the other tall, and as the tall one cleared his throat and held up a badge, he pointed to the bird poop. "Did you know that the governor of the great State of New York, in his eternal wisdom, has introduced a poop tax? And according to our records, you haven't paid."

Maybe Jeff had a point when he fled Hampton Cove. It is one crazy town!

THE END

Thanks for reading! If you want to know when a new Nic Saint book comes out, sign up for Nic's mailing list: nicsaint.com/news

EXCERPT FROM PURRFECT JACUZZI (MAX 86)

Chapter One

Rita MacKereth crouched down next to her car and slid her finger across the scratch that someone had made there. She cursed. A brand-new car, and already it was ruined. She glanced around and wondered who could have done this. Possibly the person who had parked next to her but was gone now. She did notice that whoever this person was had looked at her askance when she had returned from the supermarket pushing a shopping cart. Possibly figuring she had parked too close to her own car. But then she couldn't help it. It wasn't her fault that the powers that be made these parking slots so tiny that people had a hard time slipping in and avoiding bumping into the next car.

She rose again and shook her blond mane. Looked as if she'd have to make a trip to the garage again. Last week it had been someone hitting her rear fender when she was having her nails done at the salon, and now this. The people at the garage would give her a funny look—again!

She got into her car and was about to back out of the

EXCERPT FROM PURRFECT JACUZZI (MAX 86)

parking space when she heard a sort of crunching sound and closed her eyes in dismay. Getting out, she saw she had accidentally backed into another car, this one of the more expensive variety. A BMW. The driver was already getting out of his car and judging from the look on his face and the color of that same face, he wasn't happy with this state of affairs.

She held up her hands in a bid to stave off a possible case of road rage. "I'm so sorry. I didn't see you there."

"No, I got that!" said the guy with some irritation, but then much to her surprise she saw that his face was still as red as it had been before, or possibly even redder, but that the look of rage had morphed into one of astonishment. And as his eyes dipped down her body and clocked her curvy shape with a certain relish, she understood what was going on here.

From an early age, she'd had that effect on men, and even though it had often been annoying to say the least, especially when her classmates had behaved like hormonal teenagers around her—possibly because they had been hormonal teenagers—she had also derived certain benefits from the effect she had on the opposite sex. Like now, for instance, with this hapless BMW driver, victim of a moment's carelessness on her part.

"Let's exchange insurance information, shall we?" she said therefore, and ducked into her glove compartment to collect the leather wallet filled with the necessary paperwork for these contingencies. When she re-emerged from the car, she saw that the man was still glued to the same spot he had been before, and staring at her all googly-eyed. As she walked up to him, she tripped over a piece of detritus and in an effort to regain her balance, accidentally stepped on the man's toe.

"Ow!" he yelled. "Owowow!"

"I'm so sorry!" she cried, horrified.

"It's... all right," he groaned.

EXCERPT FROM PURRFECT JACUZZI (MAX 86)

"I'm not normally this clumsy."

"Good to know," he said as he ground his teeth in pain.

"So... do you have your papers?" she asked him.

"Yes, yes, yes," he said, and hobbled to his BMW to retrieve the documents. He was a bespectacled man in his early thirties, and quite good-looking, she thought. Not that it mattered, of course. Moments later they were exchanging information and filling out the necessary paperwork, with the man darting the occasional glance in her direction when he thought she wasn't looking—and even when he thought she was. But in spite of the fact that she was relieved he hadn't gone all Incredible Hulk on her, she decided to ignore his glances and get through this awkwardness as fast as possible.

The moment he had moved his car, she was off at a speed that must have surprised him, judging by the strange look on his face as she pulled out past him and was gone.

The last thing she needed was to get involved with random strangers that she met by bumping into them. Her love life was complicated enough as it was, with her recently discovering she was pregnant, and trying to work up the courage to tell her boyfriend about it. She hoped he would welcome the news, though she didn't hold out much hope, as they hadn't been getting along all that well lately, or in fact at all. If he didn't respond well to the news he was going to be a dad, she might be forced to bring this baby into the world as a single mom. Then again, since her own mom had been a single mom, she knew it could be done. Nevertheless, if Harvey wanted give their relationship another chance, that would probably be for the best—both for her and the baby.

She placed her hand on her belly and smiled. Even if Harvey wasn't prepared to give them another chance, she knew things would be fine. Odd how such a tiny little thing,

EXCERPT FROM PURRFECT JACUZZI (MAX 86)

no bigger than a pea according to the gynecologist during her check-up, could make such a big change in every respect.

She indicated left and soon was cruising along the main road into town. Which is when she became aware that a car was right on her tail, and behaving very dangerously and very strangely, honking its horn and flashing its lights as if to tell her something. When she glanced in the rear-view mirror, she saw to her surprise that it was the same BMW she had hit at the supermarket parking lot. And the man behind the wheel was the same man who hadn't been able to keep his eyes off her.

She wondered if she shouldn't simply ignore him. For all she knew, he might have had second thoughts about amicably arranging things between them and without involving the police. But then again, he hadn't come across as a weirdo or a homicidal maniac, and so she parked the car on the shoulder of the road and got out to see what the guy wanted this time.

"Miss MacKereth," he said, kind of breathlessly, and smiling a wide smile. He was holding something in his hand, and she now saw that it was her bag, which contained her wallet and all her personal stuff. "You forgot this," he added as he handed over the bag.

"Oh, god," she said as she took the cherished item from the man's hands. "Thank you so much. I hadn't even noticed."

"It was on the hood of your car, and when you drove off, it fell to the ground," he specified as he rocked back on his heels, looking extremely pleased with himself. He jerked his finger in the direction she had been going. "Driving home, huh?"

She smiled. "How did you guess?" She wondered if he had gone through her stuff, but then realized that he must have gleaned her address from the insurance documents.

"I also live in Hampton Cove," he intimated, suddenly

looking extremely shy. "Close to the library, in fact." When she didn't volunteer the information on where she lived, even though he probably knew, he must have realized that small talk wasn't on the cards today. And held up his hand. "Well, I must be off now. Open my store. See you around, Miss MacKereth."

"Yeah, see you around," she said, though she sincerely hoped that wouldn't be the case.

Five minutes later, she was passing the sign that said, "Welcome to Hampton Cove," and once again found her thoughts drifting to the same idle speculation about Harvey's reaction to the news that he was about to become a dad. She bit her lower lip. Even though she sincerely hoped he would be over the moon, like she was, she had to consider the fact that he might not react too favorably. Lately he'd been in such a lousy mood that anything was possible. But however he reacted, he needed to be told. His reaction would tell her whether she would be raising this baby all by herself or with the baby's daddy by her side. She truly hoped for the latter.

Chapter Two

For some reason I found hard to grasp, Dooley and Brutus were locked in a staring contest and had been for the past five minutes. The entire concept, as I understood it, revolved around the capacity to look someone in the eye without blinking. The person who blinked first, lost. And since thus far neither Brutus nor Dooley were giving an inch, the outcome was still up in the air.

Surrounding the two competitors, a sort of supporters' club had sprung up, consisting of myself, Harriet, Fifi, and Rufus. In other words: the collected pets of Harrington Street numbers 42 to 44. The place to be was our backyard, and tickets hadn't been sold, nor had the match been

EXCERPT FROM PURRFECT JACUZZI (MAX 86)

announced on social media, or else the entire neighborhood might have come out to see the show.

"I don't think this is healthy, Max," said Harriet as she squeezed my arm a little too tightly, I felt. "I mean, the eyes need lubrication, don't they? What if they suffer permanent damage from this silly nonsense?"

"I'm sure it won't be as bad as that," I assured her. "The eyes can go without lubrication for quite a while without suffering adverse effects."

"But what if the tissue shrivels up and dies, Max?" she insisted. "It happens, you know. The eyes need that tear fluid or they will DIE!"

"I don't think that's the case," said Rufus as he blinked a few times. "I think the eyes are very strong and don't need any tear fluid at all. In fact, I think that if Brutus and Dooley keep this up, they can go on for days, maybe even weeks."

"They'll need to be fed," said Fifi. "If they want to do this for days, I mean. And someone will need to make sure they get a bathroom break." She sniffed Dooley's butt, and nodded sagely. "I think he's good. Nothing seems to be coming down the pike just yet."

I rolled my eyes, and made sure to lubricate them in the process, as I'm not a big believer in torturing oneself for the pleasure of besting a fellow cat at some silly game. "Look, this will all be over within minutes," I assured my friends. "Nobody can keep their eyes open for days or weeks. It's simply not possible."

"And a good thing, too," said Harriet as she gave Rufus a stern-faced look of reproach. "Putting these silly ideas in pets' heads," she said as she shook her head. "If Brutus ruins his eyes, I'm blaming you, you know," she said in no uncertain terms.

"Eh?" said Rufus.

EXCERPT FROM PURRFECT JACUZZI (MAX 86)

"Yes, you!" said Harriet fiercely. "This was your idea in the first place."

"It wasn't! All I said was that humans sometimes like to play silly games. Like arm wrestling or trying to see who can pee the farthest. And also a staring contest."

"And now see what happened," said Harriet.

"Good thing they didn't try to see who could pee the farthest," said Fifi. "Imagine if they did that? Your lawn wouldn't like it, Max."

"It isn't technically my lawn, Fifi," I said. "But I share your sentiment."

"I think the lawn *would* like it," said Rufus. "Peeing on the lawn is good for the grass. It will make it grow at least twice as fast. Or at least that's what Ted always said," he added quickly, before he could be accused of putting ideas in cats' heads again.

"Ted pees on his own lawn?" asked Fifi.

"He does," said Rufus. "Only he does it when Marcie isn't looking, you know. I don't think she would like it."

We all shared a look of surprise. "So Ted pees on his own lawn?" I asked, just to make sure I hadn't misheard.

Rufus nodded. "He does it early in the morning, when Marcie is still asleep. And he makes sure he pees on a different part of the lawn every morning, to make sure that every blade of grass gets equal benefit of this liquid of the gods, as he calls it."

We all smiled at this. Only Ted could call his urine the liquid of the gods. But then the man had always been slightly eccentric.

"I personally blame it on being an accountant," said Rufus. "Sitting there poring over those numbers every day from morning till night, and that for however many years, must have messed with his head. Scrambled his brain, you know."

We all nodded in agreement. I found it hard to imagine

EXCERPT FROM PURRFECT JACUZZI (MAX 86)

that a person would willingly sit in front of a computer entering numbers and crunching data all his life. It sounded like torture.

"I think my snuggle bear is going to win," Harriet said. "Just look at him. Fully focused and not giving an inch. Poor Dooley. He never stood a chance."

"Don't say that," said Fifi. "I see what you're doing, Harriet, and it's not going to work."

"What am I doing?" asked Harriet.

"Psychological warfare!" said Fifi. "You're trying to turn the odds in favor of your boyfriend, and it's not fair."

Harriet's jaw had dropped out of sheer indignation. "I did no such thing!"

"It's practically tantamount to cheating," said Fifi, not pulling her punches. "And I won't stand for it. As the official referee of this battle, I'm telling you to stand down."

Harriet's mouth closed with a soft click and she gave Fifi furious looks, but she did comply and didn't try to sway the competition in Brutus's favor. Instead, she now started staring Dooley in the eyes as well, moving behind Brutus to add more stress to my friend. Fifi wasn't fooled, though, and as she gestured to Harriet to stop doing that, the white Persian finally relented and returned to her position on the sidelines, just like the rest of us.

I couldn't really tell if Dooley was in trouble or not. He didn't seem to be weakening, that was for sure. I could tell that Brutus had a hard time keeping his eyes open though, for his eyelids were trembling, and his eyes were watering. Finally, he uttered a loud cry of anguish and squeezed his peepers tightly shut.

"I'm sorry, but I can't take it anymore!" he cried, much to Harriet's dismay.

"Oh, pookie!" she cried. "Why give up now? You almost had him!"

EXCERPT FROM PURRFECT JACUZZI (MAX 86)

We all glanced at Dooley, and he certainly didn't look like a cat who was about to flinch. In fact, he was still looking straight ahead of him, and so I got the impression that he hadn't even noticed that he had won.

Who had noticed was Fifi, for she grabbed our friend's paw and held it up in the air. "Winner of this competition: Dooley!"

Suddenly Dooley seemed to wake up from some kind of slumber, which wasn't possible, since his eyes had been open the entire time. "Hm?" he said, and shook his head. "I think I fell asleep. What did I miss?"

"But Dooley," I said. "You can't have fallen asleep. Your eyes were open!"

He yawned. "Oh, didn't you know? I can sleep with my eyes open. Not sure why, though I remember that my dad could do the same. Mom always said it was a little creepy, for she would wake up in the middle of the night and think my dad was awake and would start talking to him, only to realize ten minutes in that he was still asleep. Made her feel silly."

We all laughed, except for Brutus, who gave our friend a look of dismay. "So… you were asleep this entire time?"

"Not at first, no," said Dooley. "But after a while I got bored, and I must have dozed off."

The big black cat shook his head. "That's so not fair."

"Oh, but you should try it," said Dooley. "It's very easy. You just sleep but keep your eyes open."

And since cats are naturals at trying out new things, we all tried to do what Dooley had just described. Try as I might, though, I simply couldn't do it. The moment I started to doze off, my eyes invariably closed of their own accord. It was the darnedest thing.

"I can't do it," Harriet confessed.

"Me neither," said Brutus as he blinked a few times to

EXCERPT FROM PURRFECT JACUZZI (MAX 86)

prevent his eyes from going all dry and atrophying, just like Harriet had predicted would happen.

"I can do it, you guys!" said Rufus. He had closed his eyes and looked triumphant. "See? My eyes are open, and I'm fast asleep!"

"First of all, you're not asleep since you're talking to us," said Fifi. "And second, your eyes are closed, buddy boy."

"No, but they're... Oh, gee, I guess you're right," said the big sheepdog. "Bummer."

Dooley yawned. "I guess that nap wasn't long enough. I think I'll go and lie down some." And with these words, he trotted off in the direction of the pet flap and moments later was gone.

"You know, we could probably monetize this skill," said Harriet thoughtfully.

"What skill, what are you talking about?" asked Brutus, whose eyes were still watering from the ordeal he had suffered.

"Well, Dooley's capacity to sleep with his eyes open, of course. I'll bet people would pay good money to watch a TikTok video of him demonstrating this unique skill."

I smiled as I imagined people watching a YouTube video of a cat just sitting there with his eyes open. Like watching paint dry. But when I told Harriet, she wasn't impressed.

"It's ASMR and it's a thing, Max," she assured me. "It's very relaxing to watch paint dry. In fact it's all the rage. And since people are all stressed out lately, a video of Dooley sleeping with his eyes open would be a big hit, just you wait and see." With these words, she hurried in after Dooley, possibly hoping to convince him to star in said video.

I turned to Fifi. "What's ASMR?" I asked, feeling silly for having to ask the question.

"Oh, it's videos of the wind rustling in the trees," she said. "Snails creeping through the grass. Water babbling in a

EXCERPT FROM PURRFECT JACUZZI (MAX 86)

brook. Fire crackling in the hearth. Peaceful sounds, you know."

"Okay," I said, even though I still failed to see the big attraction. But then I guess I'm not as *au courant* as I would like to be sometimes. The world does move at a rapid pace, and it's hard to keep up.

Brutus suddenly brought his face up close to mine. "Look at my eyes, Max," he implored. "Are they all right, you think?"

I stared into my friend's eyes. "They look fine," I assured him.

"They sting, Max!" he cried as he squeezed them shut. "They sting something real bad!"

I patted him on the shoulder. "Maybe have a lie-down," I suggested. "You'll feel much better afterwards." I know I always feel refreshed after a lie-down. Which is probably why it might be my favorite thing in the world. And since I felt my advice was pretty solid, I also returned indoors to sample some of my own medicine. All this talk of ASMR had made me very sleepy.

I settled in on the couch and was asleep in seconds.

Chapter Three

Tex glanced through his bedroom window and wondered if what he was seeing could possibly be true. Out there, on the lawn, his mother-in-law was performing some kind of dance. She was wielding a soup ladle and was slicing the air with it, all the while hopping up and down like a show pony on steroids and chanting some strange song.

He even rubbed his eyes to make sure he was awake and not still asleep. But when he looked again, the woman was still there, and howling away like a banshee!

He swallowed with some difficulty. He'd always known

EXCERPT FROM PURRFECT JACUZZI (MAX 86)

that this day would come. The day that Vesta finally lost her final marble and went stir-crazy.

"Marge," he said quietly.

"Mh?" said his wife of twenty-five years from the bed, where she was reading *Star Magazine* about the latest juicy gossip from the Hollywood mill.

"Come here a minute, will you?"

"What is it?" she asked as she languidly stretched.

It was Saturday morning, and as was the couple's habit, they liked to linger in bed a little longer than usual.

"Your mother is behaving really strangely," he said. Though 'strange' was probably an understatement for the kind of behavior Vesta was displaying.

Marge finally rose from the bed and tiptoed barefoot to the window. When she saw her mother hacking at the air with her soup ladle, she went perfectly still. "What is she doing?" she asked finally.

"I'm afraid it must have finally happened, sweetness," he said as gently as he could. To break the news to a patient that their mother or dad has gone bananas was hard enough, but having to spring that same news to his wife was even harder. But still, it had to be done. "I think your mother may have developed dementia."

"Nonsense," said Marge, wiping his words off the table in one fell swoop. "I think it's this show she saw last night."

"What show?" he asked.

"There was something on the Discovery Channel about rain dances, so she must have figured she'd try it out for herself."

He took a deep breath. "Ah," he said, and now remembered a conversation he and Vesta had had last night, where she complained that the crops were going to hell in a handbasket because of the lingering drought they had been experiencing in the area. "If this keeps up," she had told Tex,

EXCERPT FROM PURRFECT JACUZZI (MAX 86)

"Farmer Giles won't be Farmer Giles for much longer. I saw him a couple of days ago and he complained that he can't work under these conditions. His crops are going to die if we don't get some rain very soon now."

It was true that they hadn't had a drop of rain for weeks, and that there was even talk about cutting down on watering your lawn, washing your car, or filling up paddling pools if this kept up. Already their gardens were feeling the strain, and even though nobody likes rain, it was true that it had a very important role to fulfill.

Marge had opened the window and shouted, "Ma! What are you doing!"

"Can't you see? I'm doing a rain dance!" Vesta yelled back. "It's supposed to work like a charm." She held her face up to the sky, which was already a clear blue with a sun that was hoisting itself to new heights. "Nothing yet," she said after a moment. "But just you wait and see! Pretty soon now it'll start raining!" And with these words, she continued jumping around and slicing at the air with her makeshift weapon, shouting strange oaths.

Marge smiled as she closed the window. "At least while she's doing this she's not getting into trouble," she said with satisfaction. She gave her husband a kiss on the lips and moved swiftly off. "I'm taking a shower," she announced. Moments later he heard the shower running and wondered if the governor would soon forbid them to do that, too.

He certainly hoped not. He liked his shower in the morning, and the occasional bubble bath. He had even planned to purchase a jacuzzi, along with Chase, and have it installed when both their wives were out, so they could spring it on them as a surprise.

If they couldn't wash their cars or water their lawns, he guessed jacuzzis would be a big no-no, too. But since he didn't have a crystal ball, and a politician's ways are as erratic

EXCERPT FROM PURRFECT JACUZZI (MAX 86)

and unpredictable as the weather itself, he decided not to worry too much about it for now. So he picked up his wife's magazine and was soon up to date on all things Tinseltown. Which is how his son-in-law Chase found him ten minutes later.

*** * ***

"Dad," said the policeman as he surveyed the scene with his keen cop eye. Man dressed in pajamas reading *Star Magazine* in bed on a Saturday morning while his wife is taking a shower. Cozy scene, he thought. Very family-friendly. And exactly the kind of scene that had played out next door, except it was him that was taking the shower with Odelia reading *People Magazine* in bed to find out all about Oprah's latest weight loss scheme.

Tex looked up and immediately shoved the magazine under the pillow, looking caught. "Oh, hey, Chase," he said as he bounced up from the bed and into a standing position. Immediately he started doing some push-ups. "I was working out a little," he explained as he huffed and puffed his way through the exercise, obviously never having done it in his life. "Important to stay fit, you know," he said, panting heavily.

"Absolutely right," said Chase, who couldn't suppress a smile. "If you want me to give you some pointers…"

"Oh, no, that's fine," said Tex. "I got this."

"I'd only be too glad to."

"I've still got an old Richard Simmons video lying around somewhere," he assured him. "So I'm good."

"Excellent," said Chase as he took a seat on the edge of the bed. "Dad, I figure now might be a good time to talk about that jacuzzi. I mean, if we're going to do this, we probably should do it now. Before the weather turns again."

EXCERPT FROM PURRFECT JACUZZI (MAX 86)

"The weather isn't going to turn," said the doctor as he sprang up from his awkward position on the floor and did some token stretches. He gestured with his head to the window. "Haven't you seen your grandmother-in-law?"

Chase got up to take a look and nodded. "Oh, yeah. I asked her about it when I passed. She told me it's a rain dance."

"Take it from me, buddy," said his father-in-law. "When women like Vesta are starting to do rain dances, it's going to be a very long summer."

Chase smiled broadly. "Great," he said. "That means we'll have all summer to enjoy our jacuzzi, Dad."

Tex winced a little, but then seemed to see the wisdom in his son-in-law's words. "Maybe you're right. If we're going to do this, better we do it now. So what did you have in mind?"

"Well, I saw they've got one on sale at Target. And there are several great deals at Walmart, too. Quality-wise, I don't think we can go wrong by installing the exact same one Alec and Charlene got for themselves."

Tex looked up at this. "Alec and Charlene got themselves a jacuzzi?"

"They did," Chase confirmed. "And a great one, too. Though Alec hasn't invited me yet to try it out, I keep seeing great things about it."

Tex's face had taken on a thoughtful look. "He hasn't invited me either," he said, rubbing his chin. "I wonder why that is."

"He probably wants to enjoy it a little longer before he starts inviting others over," Chase suggested. "But I know for a fact that he and Charlene have been soaking in that thing every night for weeks now. It's all over the police station WhatsApp."

"Is that so?" said Tex, and he didn't look happy about it. Which was only to be understood, as the doctor believed in

EXCERPT FROM PURRFECT JACUZZI (MAX 86)

sharing the spoils of his own modest success with the rest of his family, and assumed that they would return the favor. Only Alec and Charlene clearly didn't feel that same way.

"Look, why don't we check it out later today? I'm sure Alec will agree. And then if we like it, we can get us the exact same model," Chase suggested.

Tex nodded. "Great idea, Chase," he said, his voice a little choked up now. "Set it up."

He clapped the man on the shoulder. "Oh, don't be like that, Dad. I'm sure it's just an oversight on Alec's part. Or maybe Charlene doesn't like it when her husband's family is all over their brand-new jacuzzi. You know what Charlene is like sometimes."

Tex nodded, but he still seemed to feel that it wasn't right to purchase an expensive new jacuzzi and not tell your family all about it and invite them over for a great evening of fun.

As he left the doctor to ruminate on this injustice, Chase hoped he hadn't stirred a hornet's nest by mentioning his boss's jacuzzi to his father-in-law. He didn't think he had, but he would still tell Alec that maybe now was a good time to invite the family over. Best not to start a feud over such a silly thing.

ABOUT NIC

Nic has a background in political science and before being struck by the writing bug worked odd jobs around the world (including but not limited to massage therapist in Mexico, gardener in Italy, restaurant manager in India, and Berlitz teacher in Belgium).

When he's not writing he enjoys curling up with a good (comic) book, watching British crime dramas, French comedies or Nancy Meyers movies, sampling pastry (apple cake!), pasta and chocolate (preferably the dark variety), twisting himself into a pretzel doing morning yoga, going for a brisk walk, and spoiling his feline assistants Lily and Ricky.

He lives with his wife (and aforementioned cats) in a small village smack dab in the middle of absolutely nowhere and is probably writing his next 'Mysteries of Max' book right now.

www.nicsaint.com

Printed in Great Britain
by Amazon